'It's not so wild,' Sienna whispered.

Lex covered her hand with his and guided it to the back of his neck. 'Yet,' he muttered, and bent his head to hers.

Sienna didn't stop to think. She didn't want to think, just feel and taste and take. He'd promised her wildness. He'd deliberately sown the seeds of her need for it. Sienna parted her lips and tasted him with her tongue, a leisurely slide along the join of his lips, a request for permission to enter. She expected consent, but instead he pulled back.

'Be very sure,' he said gruffly. 'I'm not playing, Sienna.'

'Yes, you are,' she said, her gaze firmly fixed on his mouth. But right now she didn't care. 'You always do.'

'Not always,' he murmured, and set his lips to hers.

Praise for Kelly Hunter's debut novel,
WIFE FOR A WEEK:

'WIFE FOR A WEEK is an amazing debut for author Kelly Hunter. Warm and enticing, this novel sucks the reader in. The characters are engaging and entertaining with their banter, the secondary characters shine like gems and the hero's mother, effervescent… Exciting new talent Kelly Hunter has managed to produce a novel that not only whets the appetite but leaves the reader craving more. I can't wait to see what's up next!'

—*CataRomance*

WIFE FOR A WEEK was awarded Best First Category Romance of 2006 by CataRomance, and SLEEPING PARTNER was a 2008 finalist for the Romance Writers of America RITA® Award in the Best Contemporary Series Romance category!

PLAYBOY BOSS, LIVE-IN MISTRESS

BY

KELLY HUNTER

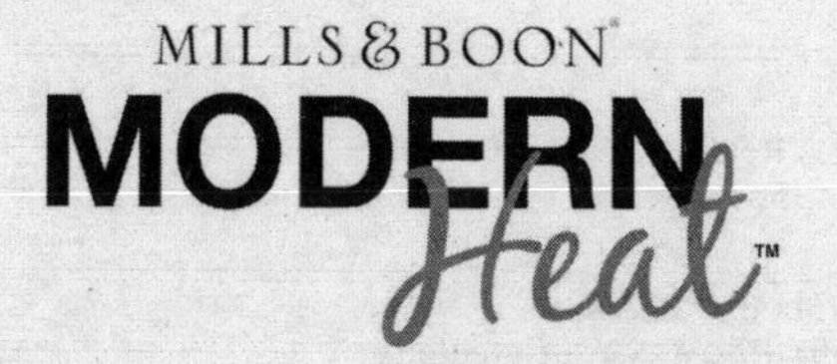

First published in Great Britain 2008
Harlequin Mills & Boon Limited,
Eton House, 18-24 Paradise Road, Richmond, Surrey TW9 1SR

ISBN: 978 0 263 86391 8

Set in Times Roman 10¾ on 12¾ pt
171-1208-47563

Printed and bound in Spain
by Litografia Rosés, S.A., Barcelona

Accidentally educated in the sciences, **Kelly Hunter** has always had a weakness for fairytales, fantasy worlds, and losing herself in a good book. Husband… yes. Children…two boys. Cooking and cleaning…sigh. Sports…no, not really—in spite of the best efforts of her family. Gardening…yes—roses, of course. Kelly was born in Australia and has travelled extensively. Although she enjoys living and working in different parts of the world, she still calls Australia home. Visit Kelly online at www.kellyhunter.net

Recent titles by the same author:

WIFE FOR A WEEK
PRICELESS
SLEEPING PARTNER
TAKEN BY THE BAD BOY

For those who dare to believe

CHAPTER ONE

ALEXANDER WENTWORTH THE THIRD could be a very patient man when he wanted to be.

Take the stock market, the money market, the futures market, *any* market, for example… When it came to waiting for the opportune moment, Lex had been known to exhibit the patience of Job.

If an eight-knot wind was blowing north-north-east off the Cornwall coast, and he had no place to be but on his yacht and nothing to do but set a course and peel a diamond-encrusted bikini off a beautiful woman, Lex could be very patient indeed. Journeys of seduction were meant to be savoured and savour them he did. Frequently.

Yes, indeed. Patience was one of Lex's many virtues.

Unfortunately, his current stock of patience was fading fast, and it wasn't just because he was fifteen hours into a twenty-five hour flight from London to Sydney, with a stopover in Singapore still pending. It was because his temporary personal assistant had a God-given talent for driving him nuts.

Sienna Raleigh was her name; personal assistant and right-hand man her latest trade. She had a doctorate in Renaissance Art, impeccable if somewhat colourful lineage, and a smile that could drop a man at fifty paces. Sienna had been five when they'd first met. Lex had been all of eleven, and her failure to acknowledge his superiority in all things had both irritated and intrigued him. He should've taken it as a warning never to employ her, he thought glumly. He really should've made an effort and crushed her insurgency some twenty years ago, the moment he'd first set eyes on her, he deduced with a sigh. Because he didn't have a hope in Hades of crushing it now.

'Any more stock reports to read?' he asked her.

'You mean apart from the dozens you've already read?' she said, without lifting her gaze from the book she was reading. 'No.'

'Any more newspapers?'

'You've read all those too.'

'Just checking.' He waited a beat. 'What's that you're reading?'

'An airport novel.' Sienna's long-suffering tone served only to amuse him. Clearly the nut-driving worked both ways. 'I'm up to the part where our hero—due to a combination of strength, determination, brilliance, luck, and fortuitous plotting—single-handedly nabs the villains and then walks away from the traitorous yet agonisingly beautiful woman who betrayed him.'

'Sounds reasonable,' he said. 'Keep me posted.' He drummed his fingers on the armrest, flicked through the entertainment channels. Sighed.

Sienna looked up at him from her book, those golden brown eyes with their tiny flecks of green revealing acute exasperation and a refreshing lack of guile. 'Admit it,' she said. 'You have the attention span of a gnat.'

'I do not.'

'And you want my book.'

'No, I don't. Unless of course you're finished with it.'

'I'm not.'

'Because it certainly sounds like the end to me.'

'There's an epilogue.'

'You actually *read* epilogues?'

'Wouldn't want to miss anything,' she said sweetly. 'Attention to detail is what you pay me for, remember? It was in the job description.'

'Wasn't catering to my every whim in the job description too?' he asked. 'I thought it was.'

'Maybe in *your* draft. Your former PA removed all references to slavery before she sent it out.'

'She *was* an uncommonly good PA,' he said on a sigh, and meant every word. 'I still don't understand how she could choose marriage and motherhood over working for me.'

'Unfathomable,' said Sienna a little too dryly for comfort.

'You like working for me, don't you?'

'Lex, I've been working for you for three days and so far it's been bedlam. I've rescheduled five meetings, changed our travel arrangements twice, kept an investment bank president on hold for fifteen minutes, begged your former PA to return on a daily basis, and vowed to shoot you at least a dozen times.'

'What can I say?' he said. 'It's been a slow week. You'll like the set-up in Australia, though. Trust me.'

Sienna ran her hand along the leather armrest and looked around the spacious cabin area as if assessing the benefits of business-class travel, before turning an amused gaze on him. 'Speaking of the set-up in Sydney…I still don't think it's a good idea for us to share a house while we're there. A month is a long time, Lex.'

'It's not a house, it's a business hub,' he said. 'And you'll have an entire wing to yourself and a commute to work of approximately fifty metres. None of my other PAs ever complained of it.'

'None of them are still working for you either. What if I want to get away from you and the work? What if I want to entertain? What if *you* want to entertain?'

'Will you have *time* to entertain?' he countered.

'Who knows?' She stood and stretched, giving him a nose to navel view of an impossibly tiny waist and firmly rounded buttocks. 'I might.'

Not if he had anything to do with it. Which—as fortune would have it—he did.

It occurred to him, not for the first time during these past few days, that Sienna might just have a point. That sharing adjoining quarters with her these next few weeks was going to prove far more of a challenge than he'd anticipated. He and Sienna hadn't seen much of one another these past few years. Different paths, different lifestyles, that was what he'd told his mother and anyone else who'd asked. Childhood friends often drifted apart, end of story, and if there was another reason he'd kept his distance lately, well, that was for him to know and no one else. When it came to Sienna, Lex's body and brain were not in alignment. His brain wanted his role in Sienna's life to be much the same as it always had been. Protector, mentor, occasional antagonist.

His body just wanted her naked beneath him. Hotly responsive. Possibly begging…

'Lex.'

Right voice, wrong tone altogether. Where was the breathless pleading? The dulcet whimpers of a woman with nothing but fulfilment on her mind?

'Alex!'

Whoa! He looked up with a start to find Sienna staring down at him in exasperation as she dangled some sort of report in front of his nose—a prospectus for a Shanghai construction company about to list on the New York stock exchange, to be exact. He'd mentioned the company in passing a couple of days ago but hadn't expected her to follow up on it. 'For me? Aw, you shouldn't have.'

'Think of it as the toy truck every mother in the known universe keeps in her handbag for when she's out and about and wants her fractious toddler to behave.' She fixed him with the queen of all challenging smiles, then picked up her book and settled back into her seat. 'Enjoy.'

'No, really. You shouldn't have. They're heavily invested in the US sub-prime housing market. They're going down.'

'Then see what you can pick up in the fire sale. Isn't that what you do?'

She had a point. She did have a point. But he didn't feel like reading any more. He needed to diffuse some of the sexual awareness currently tying him in knots, and if seduction wasn't an option—and it *wasn't*—then an argument would have to suffice. All he had to do was pick a reason, any reason. Maybe he *should* voice those mostly brotherly instincts and tell her that entertaining another man while living under his roof was out of the question. 'About us living together…'

'You mean about us occasionally meeting each other outside of working hours in common entertainment areas?' Sienna arched a delicate eyebrow and smiled a hoyden's smile. 'And what we should do if the other person has someone else with them?'

Lex smiled back, every sense sharpening beneath his lazy façade. She *did* want to fight. It would be churlish of him not to oblige. 'If you happen upon me while I'm entertaining, I will of course introduce you to my companion and quite possibly ask you to join us, at which point you will in all likelihood refuse and give me one of those looks—yes, that's the one—and take yourself off elsewhere. Does that sound reasonable?'

'Does that scenario work both ways?'

'Well…no.' He loved the way her eyes flashed fire and her chin came up. 'Should *you* wish to entertain, I'll require three days' notice and a thorough background check on the individual, or individuals, concerned. How does that sound?'

'Restrictive.'

Perfect. 'One can never be too careful. Imagine how you'd hate yourself if you were played for a fool by a reporter after an inside story on *me*. You'd be crushed. And I just know that *somehow*—in some nebulous parallel universe accessible only to the female psyche—it would be all my fault.' He shook his head sorrowfully. 'Make that five days notice. I hate being the one at fault.'

'You think I can't recognise a reporter when I see one?' she said with the quirk of an eyebrow. 'With *my* family background?'

'You're right,' he said, conceding yet another strategic point. Not a problem to his way of thinking given that the entire aim of this conversation was not necessarily to win but to fight. Sienna's mother had been many years older and several hundred million dollars wealthier than her artist husband. The press had feasted on the disparity for years, but the banquet had really started with Sienna's mother's alleged suicide. The squandered millions. The faithless husband. The forged will and the missing paintings. Two months after Sienna's mother died, her father had played chicken with a freight train and lost, and the gutter press had started up again. Eventually, thankfully, they'd moved on to newer, juicier stories but Sienna's loathing for the press and her reluctance to step anywhere near the limelight remained. 'Bad example. A reporter wouldn't last five minutes with you. But what say a thief tried to woo you in order to gain access to the complex? Know anything about thieves?'

A fleeting smile crossed the generous curve of her lips. 'People call you a thief, Lex. I know a lot about you.'

He knew what people called him. He'd heard it all before and was prepared to let the insult pass. Actually, no, he wasn't. This time the insult rankled. Time to ramp this argument up a notch. 'I pay for what I take.'

'You pay a pittance for what you take—then you break it down, repackage it, and make a fortune,' she said with brutal accuracy. 'Doesn't matter if it's legal, Lex. To some people's way of thinking, you're still a thief.'

'The technical term is corporate raider.'

'Raider, brigand, pirate…thief.' Her eyes challenged him to explain the difference. Presuming there *was* a difference.

'Those companies have been ruined by mismanagement, overextension, or plain old neglect long before I ever arrive on the scene,' he argued. 'I'm not responsible for that.'

'No,' she said. 'You're right, you're not.' Sienna opened her mouth as if to say more, but closed it again without uttering a word. She opted instead for opening her book and trying to ignore him, but he wasn't about to let her off the hook that easily. He reached over, took the book from her hands and shoved it down the side of her seat.

'Say it,' he said curtly. 'Whatever you were about to say, say it.'

Sienna looked mutinous, not to mention defensive. Lex knew from experience that following orders—his or anyone else's—was not her strong suit. But then she spoke.

'You could save those companies, Lex. Turn them around rather than tear them to pieces.'

'I *knew* that was where you were heading with this. I knew it!' He'd wanted an argument, he reminded himself bleakly. Just not this one. 'It's not that simple.'

'I realise that. But you could save them—'

'You give me far too much credit.'

'—if you wanted to,' she finished. 'You just don't want to.'

'You're right. I don't,' he murmured and felt his shoulder muscles bunch and tighten, and all because of a criticism he'd heard a thousand times before. He'd had enough of this flight. Of Sienna's criticism. Of wanting Sienna in his arms with one breath and wishing her a million miles away with his next. He'd had more than enough of that.

He half rose from his seat, trying to get past her so he could go somewhere else. Somewhere Sienna's measuring, questioning gaze wasn't, but she didn't shrink back in her seat to let him past like any normal person would do. Oh, no, she didn't do that. Now that he'd pushed her to state her case, she wanted a reply. 'This isn't about fixing other people's mistakes,' he said curtly. 'It's about capitalising on them. Darwin's theory of evolution fits the corporate business model to perfection. It's survival of the fittest, the fastest, the strongest, and the smartest. Not to mention the most ruthless.'

'Where's your sense of social responsibility?' she asked quietly.

'With me and mine.'

'Working with you these past few days has been such a revelation.' Her green on gold gaze held him prisoner; she would not back down. 'Just when you think you know a person…'

He smiled mirthlessly. 'What? You didn't think I was ruthless?'

'Not that ruthless.'

'Well, now you know.' He could have brushed past her then, would have if he hadn't made the fatal mistake of dropping his gaze to her lips, those soft, perfectly shaped lips. He leaned down, put his hands on the armrests either side of her and moved in close, until his mouth almost brushed hers. 'Want to be mine, Sienna?' he whispered with more than a lick of temper to his words.

She went perfectly still. As if she'd forgotten how to move, how to breathe. As if he were the predator and she the prey, thought Lex, and felt his body respond to the notion with savage satisfaction. Embracing it, savouring it, as simmering temper turned into a different kind of heat altogether. 'Breathe,' he whispered.

'No.' Her voice sounded thready, uncertain, and the beast inside him purred.

'You'll die if you don't.'

She took a breath and released it raggedly before easing slowly back against the seat, her startled gaze not leaving his. 'Breathing's not the problem here,' she muttered and took another shaky breath. 'I'm on it, see? But I'd rather not be yours.'

'No?' Lex smiled grimly and slid his gaze down her body. At first glance, Sienna's body language backed up her words. Her hands were ironing out the creases in her little pink skirt, smoothing the material down towards her knees as if she would have liked a couple more inches of fabric. Her knees pressed primly together, barring his way, and she'd tucked her legs tightly against the seat, demure-schoolgirl-style. Alas, there was nothing demure about her delicate pink sandals. Those shoes were all grown up.

So were other things about her.

At her throat he noticed the frantic beating of a pulse gone wild.

Outlined against her fitted white business shirt he could see the unmistakable imprint of nipples gone hard.

Sienna Raleigh, childhood nemesis and bane of his existence, was all hot and bothered. By him.

Somewhere down in the purely primal recesses of his being, Lex found the notion deeply, *deeply* satisfying. He pulled back to stare broodingly down at her. That tiny telltale reaction was going to cost her. It was going to cost them both. 'Just when you think you know a person…' he echoed softly.

Sienna was the first to look away.

'Tell me something, Sienna. If you don't like what I do for a living and you don't want to share a house with me for the next month, why the *hell* did you come to me and ask me to train you as a PA in the first place?'

'You could have said no,' she said finally, still not deigning to look at him.

'You have no idea how close I came to saying exactly that.'

'Then you should have!' She speared him with a lightning glance before looking away again quickly. 'I'd have understood.'

No, he thought. You wouldn't have. Not until I'd shown you exactly what I want from you these days. Not until now. Lex smiled tightly as the bonds of childhood friendship warred with the desires of a man well used to taking what he wanted. 'You started this,' he said softly.

'You could have said no.' Her voice was low, stricken. She knew damn well what she'd set in motion. She knew *him*. 'Why didn't you?'

'When have I ever said no to you, Sienna?' He had to get out of here, now, before he covered her lips with his own and smashed a lifelong friendship to smithereens. 'When?'

Sienna watched through hot eyes as Lex strode down the aisle away from her, her mind whirling as she replayed the events of the last few minutes. How on earth had they gone from good-natured bickering to smouldering awareness to outright warfare in the space of a few heartbeats? Lex was her *friend*. Practically the brother she'd never had. He spent half his life needling her and the other half protecting her. That was what he did. What he'd always done. That was how their relationship worked. How dared he bring his sexuality into play and use it against her? How *dared* he give her The Look.

Sienna knew that look. It had brought countless perfectly sensible, rational women to their knees, desperate for more of him.

Sometimes Lex gave more. Any lover of his could

expect a significant initial outlay of his time and attention. Rumour had it they could expect generous access to his money and possessions. Extremely generous access to his body. Unparalleled dedication to theirs.

For a time.

Until Lex had satisfied his curiosity, at which point he was gone, leaving hitherto sensible, rational women weeping in his wake, savagely cursing his focus, his stamina, and the sheer animal beauty of him, right before begging him to return.

Lex was a charming rake—just ask any woman he'd ever taken to his bed. Sienna *knew* that. Accepted it. Despised it. And for the most part ignored it—secure in the knowledge that her relationship with him was different. It always *had* been different.

Until now.

What was he doing messing with a perfectly good friendship that was manageable, mildly acerbic, and, above all, safe? Who in their right mind would throw away twenty years of friendship on a brief bedroom romp?

Not her.

So what if she'd found the full force of Lex's sexuality exhilarating? So what if she'd come closer than ever before to understanding *why* women were willing to accept Lex on his terms—on any terms—and to hell with the heartbreak? That still didn't mean she wanted to *become* one of them. No, no, and no!

Oh, look. He'd found a flight attendant. Now he was smiling crookedly at the woman; murmuring to her. Now she was smiling back. Surprise surprise.

Now Lex turned to look down the aisle towards her, a vision of careless elegance in a miraculously rumple-free business suit minus the tie. What was it about lean, dark-haired, grey-eyed men in charcoal-coloured business suits and snowy white shirts that made a woman look twice, and then—if it was Lex—again? Did his obvious wealth lend him an air of sophistication, success, and sex appeal or was it all just Lex? Would her sudden acute awareness of him disappear if she pictured him standing there in, say, grandfather pyjamas? The ones where the waistband of the trousers resided just below the armpits and the buttons went all the way to the neck. Not the sexy low-slung grey-striped cotton trousers she'd shoved in his carry on luggage yesterday. Now was definitely not the time to imagine him in those.

Oh, dear.

Sienna grabbed for the arm of a passing attendant. 'Water,' she croaked. 'Please.'

'Of course.' The attendant took one look at her and decided to hustle. Did she look pale? She felt ashen. Did she look ill? She felt as if the world had suddenly tilted off its axis and no matter what she did she couldn't set it right again. She didn't *want* Lex to look at her like that. She didn't want to be one of his conquests.

Did she?

Lex started down the aisle and Sienna quickly looked away and braced herself for his return to a seat that was suddenly far too close to hers for comfort. She tucked her legs against her seat as Lex swept past her. Keep going, Lex, well done, breathe out.

'Good news,' he said as he settled into his seat, his voice casual, as if he'd decided to forget all about their earlier altercation. 'We're landing in Singapore in twenty minutes. We can go into the terminal. Stretch our legs, stock up on airport novels and newspapers. There's an executive lounge area that has internet access. Showers too.'

'So much to do, so little time,' she said, but she was grateful for both the impending stopover and Lex's efforts to put their relationship back on its normal footing. Forgetting all about the upheavals of the last ten minutes was a mighty fine plan to her way of thinking. Being able to get away from Lex for a spell was an even better idea. 'You shop, I'll shower.'

'A good PA would stay by my side and see to my needs,' he said.

She knew the basic philosophy but even so… 'Even in transit?'

'Especially in transit.' Lex smiled grimly. He'd been doing that a lot lately. 'Maybe it's a good thing I *was* prepared to take you on and train you up. Imagine if you'd taken that job with the oil sheik in Dubai? OPEC would never have been the same again.'

'The sheik didn't think I'd make a mess,' she said tartly. '*He* thought I could do it.'

'The sheik was besotted with you, Sienna,' said Lex darkly.

Unfortunately, Lex was correct. It was one of the reasons she hadn't taken the job. The other reason, and it galled her to admit it, had been her lack of experience in all matters pertaining to the business of being a good personal assistant. She'd needed experience. Lex had needed an assistant for a month while he was in Australia. Sienna had no aversion whatsoever to visiting the colonies. Sienna had long overdue personal business she could attend to while in Australia. The entire plan had seemed like such a good idea.

At the time.

'Thank you for agreeing to this, Lex,' she said awkwardly. 'I do appreciate it. Really. And I didn't mean to question your business ethics, earlier. I just...wanted to understand.'

'And now that you do?' He looked wary. Defensive. 'Do you still want to be my PA for the month, Sienna?'

'Yes.' She shoved her newfound awareness of him aside, took another deep breath and collected her scattered wits. 'If you're skilful enough to take bits and pieces of broken companies and put them together in ways that work, then I'm all for it. I was in fix-it mode before. Now I'm thinking salvage. Corporate recycling. I'm all for recycling.'

'Recycling,' he said disbelievingly.

'Absolutely.' She offered up a smile for good measure.

'You've missed your calling,' he told her. 'Corporate public relations needs you.'

Sienna felt her smile widen. This was the Lex she knew and understood. *This* Lex she could handle. 'So what exactly is it that you want me to *do* while we're in transit?'

He stared at her through narrowed assessing eyes and Sienna stared back with as much calm as she could muster. After what seemed like an eternity Lex bestowed on her a smile an angel would've been proud of. He was up to something. Nothing surer.

'Tell you what...' he said graciously. 'I'll shower, you hold the towel.'

CHAPTER TWO

TWENTY minutes later the plane touched down in Singapore and Sienna preceeded Lex along narrow non-descript corridors towards the transit lounge. She felt a lot better now that they were off the plane—more in control of herself and her surroundings. Far more inclined to think that her and Lex's sensually loaded altercation had been nothing more than edginess and boredom on his part and a never-to-be repeated moment of insanity on hers.

Sienna's internal clock told her it was long past her bedtime, but the arrival and departure boards inside the terminal said it was six p.m. and the light outside the windows confirmed it. She was tired, she realised belatedly. Add that to the list of reasons for her strange reaction to Lex. She added it to his side of the equation too. The hours he'd worked during these last few days leading up to the trip had been phenomenal. *And* there hadn't been a beautiful companion in sight. Not for months, according to her godmother, Adriana, who also happened to be Lex's mother. Sienna added 'overdue' to Lex's list of reasons for uncharacteristic behaviour. Wonderful things, lists.

The standard array of shops graced the terminal corridors. Coffee bar, newsagent, chain-store music and books, lotions, potions, and soap… Wait! Soap. Gorgeously scented luxury soap. To use in the shower… Sienna stopped abruptly and Lex all but crashed into her in the process.

'What did you forget?' he said.

'Nothing.' He of little faith. 'I just want some soap.'

'I already have soap.'

'Why is it always about you?'

'It just…usually is.'

'Well, not this time.' Honestly, the man had been thoroughly indulged for far too long. 'The soap is for me.'

'My mistake.' Lex wandered over to the nearest display. 'What kind of soap do you want?'

'I'll know it when I smell it,' she said.

'I see.' His expression said he didn't understand the delights of scented-soap shopping at all. 'What say we forgo your PA training for the next couple of hours and I meet you back on the plane?' But the ancient Asian saleswoman had already made her move.

'Come. Come,' she said, waving them into the shop proper. 'It is good for the man to choose the soap for the woman. Choose now, benefit later, no?'

'No,' said Sienna, but the saleswoman ignored her.

'This one,' she said, and handed Lex a block of soap. 'Ylang ylang and lemongrass. Smell good, no?'

Lex sniffed. Considered. Decided. And all without giving Sienna a second glance. 'No,' he said as he handed the soap back to the woman. 'She's more of a rosehip kind of girl.'

'I am not!' said Sienna.

'Rosehip and vanilla?' said the saleswoman, picking up another block of soap and offering it to him. 'This one you like?'

'Hello,' said Sienna. 'Over here.'

'Got anything with ginger in it?' said Lex.

'Sandalwood and ginger,' said the woman and passed that one to him as well. 'Also matching body lotion, hand cream, and shampoo.'

'Sold,' said Lex and produced a wallet from his trouser pocket. 'Don't bother wrapping it.'

'How sweet,' murmured Sienna. 'You think we're done here.'

'We are done here.' He strode towards the register. 'You wanted soap. You got soap. And moisturiser, and shampoo. What more could you possibly need?'

This wasn't about need. It was about shopping. Possibly about revenge. 'There's a men's range.'

'No,' he said hastily.

'Oh, yes.' Sienna studied him serenely. If he thought he could treat her like a charity case and pick up the tab for her expenses he was mistaken. She wasn't on the poverty line yet. She could still afford soap.

The saleswoman studied him too. 'So much hurry,' she said. 'Does he have airplane to catch?'

'He just got off one.' Lex opened his mouth to speak. 'He's about to tell you he already has soap,' Sienna murmured. 'Anyone would think he's not a patient man.'

'A man with no patience is like an ocean without fish,' said the woman, and continued to study Lex. 'Why even cast the net?'

'I have fish,' said Lex indignantly. 'I have plenty of fish.'

'Of course you do.' Sienna couldn't quite hide her smirk. Who'd have thought there'd be such joy to be had in a transit terminal soap shop?

'Allspice and lemon thyme?' offered the saleswoman.

Close. There was no denying the man's edibility, although she fully intended to. 'I'm thinking cinnamon.'

'Cinnamon and orange,' said the woman, picking up a nearby block of soap and handing it to her. 'Good choice.'

Sienna took it. Sniffed it. 'I don't know… I'm not sure…' And with devilry in mind she said, 'He may need to try it on.'

'How—?' he began, and then spied the basin and tap. 'No.'

Oh, yes. 'I'd hate to choose wrong. Imagine if the aroma didn't complement your manly essence?'

'Sienna, it's *soap*.'

'How little you know,' she said and reached for his arm, pushing his jacket sleeve up to his elbow before taking his wrist and turning it to expose the inside of his forearm. 'Think of the fish.'

The saleswoman slapped a damp cloth on his skin and deftly wet him from elbow to wrist. 'The soap will slide,' she said.

The soap did slide. And somewhere between elbow and wrist Sienna lost the upper hand and Lex found it.

'Now you rub with your hands,' the saleswoman told her. 'I take the soap.'

Lex's mouth curved lazily and his eyes gleamed. 'I like a firm touch,' he murmured.

He got one and winced, doubtless from pleasure.

'She's so obliging,' he told the saleswoman. 'Really. Ouch!'

'A woman without spirit is like a sky with no clouds,' said the woman.

'Perfect?' said Lex.

'No. Such a sky will never quench your thirst.'

'Isn't that what bottled water's for?' said Lex, and winced some more as Sienna's thumb accidentally encountered another soft spot. 'Easy, sweetheart. You're bruising the goods.'

'Sorry.' Sienna trailed her fingernails lightly down his arm, leaving a row of wavy snakelike tracks in the lather. Lex shuddered ever so slightly and his eyes flashed a heated warning.

'Keep it up, Sienna, and you will be.'

Oh, dear. There it was again—exhilaration, illumination, and a powerful curiosity about what Lex might bring to a sexual relationship—all of it coalescing into a tight ball of sensation deep in the pit of her stomach. Sienna moved to the sink, washed the soap from her hands and stood back to let Lex wash his arm, acutely aware that lathering him in cinnamon soap hadn't been one of her better ideas.

She wasn't six any more; Lex wasn't her indulgent older playmate.

She wasn't a skinny, smart-mouthed fifteen-year-old any more either; Lex wasn't her confidante and protector.

Lex dried his hands and arms with a paper towel and turned towards her, every movement a subtle challenge, and Sienna realised with blinding clarity that those days were over.

He put his forearm to his nose, took a whiff, shrugged, and held his arm up towards her, those knowing grey eyes daring her to play out the scene to completion. Maybe she ought to add 'too easily led' to her side of the equation, she thought wryly, because she knew instinctively that breathing him in was going to cost her control she could ill afford to lose. But she closed her eyes and breathed deeply anyway.

The aroma of cinnamon came first, then citrus, then Lex. The ache in her stomach pulled tighter.

'How does it combine with my manly essence?' he murmured, his voice a low, husky rumble that sounded like sin and burned like the devil.

'Quite well,' she whimpered, her eyes still tightly closed.

'I was aiming a little higher than quite well.' Had he moved closer? Was it his body that was on fire or was it hers? Because something here was burning, nothing surer. Something brushed her ear and she shivered hard. His hair, she thought at first. No, maybe his cheek. His lips… 'Maybe we should try a different soap on the other arm,' he whispered.

Sienna stumbled back a step and opened her eyes and immediately wished she hadn't. There it was again: The Look. And Lex didn't look tired or edgy or in any way bored. He looked focussed and sexy as hell and the reckless hunger in his eyes called to needs she'd never known she had. 'No need to try another one on,' she said, adding a weak smile for good measure. 'This one combines very well.'

'I appreciate the adverbial upgrade,' he countered with a lazy grin. 'But the fact remains that the basic assessment is mediocre. Are you sure you don't want to make me try on another one?'

'It lifts your manly essence into the realms of the sublime,' she practically yelled. 'I am trembling with lust.'

'I think she likes it,' Lex told the lady. 'I'll take a month's worth.'

Sienna fled Lex's company after that and Lex let her. The scent of cinnamon and orange soap and Lex the marauder stayed in her mind and on her hands until there was nothing for it but to shower it off, wash it straight down the drain, and replace it with plain old airport hotel soap and shampoo, never mind the gorgeous goodies from the soap shop burning a hole in her handbag. Even then her mind strayed as she lathered up and scrubbed hard. She imagined a man's hands on her, but not just any man's hands. These were knowing hands, demanding hands.

Lex's hands.

'Why me?' she whimpered. Why Lex? 'Why *now*?'

Oh, there'd been that time on her eighteenth birthday when Lex had commandeered her for a slow dance at the end of the evening and she'd been a mass of nerves for fear he was planning to kiss her, but that had been years ago. Besides, he hadn't. Not on the lips. He'd kissed her temple instead, told her to watch out for Bobby Carmichael's wandering hands, and left with the beautiful blonde events manager that Adriana had hired to oversee the evening.

The beautiful blonde hadn't lasted a week.

Neither had Bobby Carmichael.

Then there'd been that time when Lex had turned up at her flat one morning and the very sweet Aidan Russell had chosen that particular moment to wander out of her bedroom. Lex hadn't liked coming face to face with Sienna's love life, never mind that his own had spanned three continents by then, the ice in his eyes could have frozen the Thames. After about two minutes of stilted conversation, including introductions, Aidan had become visibly nervous.

Aidan hadn't lasted long either.

How many years ago was that? Two? Three? There'd

been no one for Sienna since then. Sighing, Sienna added 'long overdue' to her list of reasons for her sudden uncomfortable awareness of Lex's manly attractions and tilted her face beneath the spray. Moments later visions of Lex in the shower with her—with his hands on her—began to assail her. She turned the cold tap on full and concentrated on getting clean rather than aroused, but occasionally an image stuck and when it did it ripped into her with cyclone force. Her body bowed and her skin ached for a lover's touch.

A *lover's* touch, she told herself fiercely. Not Lex's touch.

Any lover would do. There was such a thing as taking the edge off.

And then her relationship with Lex would be the same as it always had been. Sacrosanct.

Sienna emerged from the shower feeling suitably clean but in no way relaxed. The thought of Lex showering with *his* soap and Sienna having to sit next to him on the plane for another eight hours, breathing him in, wasn't a reassuring one to a woman whose body ached for fulfilment and whose mind had remained back in London. If he turned that lazy charm on her again, heaven forbid if he touched her, she was likely to implode. Lex would probably find it amusing. Sienna didn't find the notion amusing at all.

Think, Sienna, think. She'd known this man for most of her life. She knew his strengths and all his flaws. She knew full well that he was only amusing himself with her on account of a distinct lack of anything else amusing at hand. The obvious solution, therefore, was to find something else for him to focus on.

She hit the shops again and bought him a book. An adventure story with ticking bombs and many villains. That'd doubtless keep him occupied for, oh…five minutes. She bought him a book of mastermind sudoku puzzles. That'd hold him for longer. What else? A major crisis of confidence on Wall Street would be good. She skimmed the newspapers for just such an occurrence, but it wasn't to be. What else would a good PA collect for her boss before getting back on that plane?

Probably her composure.

Definitely her wits.

Her resolve to not become romantically involved with old friends, new bosses, or millionaire playboys for whom romance was just a diversion. Which pretty much ruled Lex out on all counts.

The final boarding call came about far too quickly and Sienna stepped gingerly back inside the plane, armed to the teeth with distractions, only to find Lex already seated, with his computer open on his lap. His gaze was penetrating but his smile was the one from their childhood as she tucked her purchases into the webbing of the seat in front of her and her carry bag into the locker above. She settled into her seat and took a tentative breath. No cinnamon or orange. Lex had showered—his hair was still damp—but not with his new soap.

Hallelujah.

Lex shut down his laptop for take-off, his impatience a tangible force, those long, lean fingers drumming rhythmically on the slim machine, his gaze distracted and far away.

'Something I should know about?' she queried, feeling ever so slightly guilty that she hadn't stuck with him during the stopover.

'The breakdown of the Scorcellini assets has come

in,' said Lex. 'They're in surprisingly good shape for a company going under.'

'Is this a good thing?'

'It is for them. Means their chances of attracting a rescue bid are higher than I thought.'

'So where does that leave your bid?'

'In need of readjustment.' He shot her a glance. 'You're not going to suggest that I rescue them?'

'No. I have a new approach when it comes to dealings of a financial nature. I won't criticise your decisions.'

'I like it,' he said.

'And you don't criticise mine.'

'You had to go and spoil it.'

'Do we have a deal?'

'No.' He smiled crookedly. 'Criticise away. I may not always like or agree with what you have to say, Sienna, but I still want to hear it.'

Sienna sighed heavily. Now he was being charming. 'Would you want to hear the opinions of a PA you *hadn't* known since childhood?'

'Probably not. But, then, you're not a regular employee, are you? Which means some of the regular rules simply don't apply. I can give you the workload a PA would get from me. I can show you how to do it. But don't ask me to treat you like a proper PA this coming month because I can't.'

'You could try.'

'And I'd fail. I don't look to you for instant obedience, Sienna. I look to you for truth.'

Sienna went all marshmallow-soft inside; she couldn't help it.

The seat-belt lights went off. Lex opened his laptop

and started opening files. 'And trouble,' he muttered. 'Trust me, Sienna, you bring that to the table too.'

At five fifty-five a.m., local time, Sienna and Lex stepped off the plane, collected their luggage, cleared customs, and stepped into the arrivals area. Sienna had never been to Australia before. The dress code of the people waiting for passengers seemed far more informal than that of the people at Heathrow. People smiled more and walked slower, the air was warmer and the general vibe felt a whole lot more relaxed.

Or maybe she only thought it felt more relaxed because she was so glad to finally get off that plane. Lex had focussed on his work for most of the Singapore-Sydney leg of the trip, stopping only for meal breaks. There had been no awkward moments of heart-stopping sexual tension, nothing out of the ordinary at all, not on Lex's part at any rate. But Sienna still hadn't quite been able to relax in his company. Not until they'd left the plane behind.

'The trick to jet lag and adjusting quickly to the new time zone is to stay awake for the rest of the day, local time, and crawl into bed around midnight,' Lex told Sienna as he collected both his suitcases and hers.

'Uh-huh,' Sienna replied with increasing good humour as they strode through the glass doors and out onto the Sydney pavement. Fresh air, heavily laden with exhaust fumes and the promise of a hot summer's day, greeted her. 'It sounds perfectly sensible in *theory*, don't get me wrong. Remind me again when I fall asleep in my soup at lunchtime. How far is it to your place from here, again?'

'Half an hour.' Lex steered the bags towards a waiting

limousine, gave the driver the address and opened the back door for Sienna to get in. 'Watson's Bay lies just inside the southern entrance to Sydney Harbour. The land there tapers off to a point, with one side facing the bay and the other side facing the ocean. It's a nice spot. You'll like it,' he told her with a boyish smile that told of his enthusiasm for his latest cubbyhole. He'd always had dozens of special places tucked away in the grounds of his family's estate as a child. Sienna had delighted in seeking them out during her visits, and Lex had always shared them with her with good grace and enthusiasm, just as he was doing now. It had taken her years before she'd realised that Lex was a whole lot more careful about sharing himself with anyone else. He'd grown up wary of reporters and social climbers; people who saw the money and the position in society rather than the man, never mind that the man himself was spectacular.

If she could just think of this Sydney home as Lex's latest cubby rather than the abode of a man who could damage her calm with nothing more than a single heated glance, they would get along just fine. 'And the house?' she questioned. 'The hub? Which side is it on?'

'The bay side. I needed somewhere to put the yacht.'

'Of course,' she said dryly. 'The yacht.'

'There's a housekeeper too. His name's Rudy. He used to be a Navy frigate midshipman. He likes things tidy. Cooks extremely tasty French frou-frou food but you might want to stay out of his kitchen. He's territorial.'

'Pity. I like kitchens.' Kitchens had been her refuge as a child, especially when her parents had been mid-argument, which had been most of the time. She tended to gravitate towards them, even as an adult. A boiling kettle and the fixings for a cup of tea provided comfort and warmth on too many levels to count.

Lex sent her a sharp glance but stayed silent.

'Is the presence of Rudy the former frigate midshipman supposed to be reassuring when it comes to the thought of sharing a house with you for a month?' she said next.

'I figured it would be,' he said mildly.

'What if *he* wants to entertain?'

'Don't dwell on it. I never do. Rudy lives in the apartment over the garage. What he does there is his business.' And at her raised eyebrow he added, 'All I'm saying is that we're not going to be entirely alone in the house, that's all. You might want to factor that into your decision-making process.'

'Thanks. I will.' Sienna chewed pensively on her bottom lip. She didn't want to be contrary or difficult. She just wanted the month to go as smoothly as possible. 'In the interests of exploring all options, have you any idea how expensive the rents nearby would be?'

'Expensive,' he said. 'Watson's Bay isn't a budget area, Sienna.'

'What about housing a little further away?'

'Then the commute will be longer.'

'It's called compromise.'

'I know what compromise is,' he said curtly. 'The business world is full of it. What I don't understand is why you feel the need to make such a compromise.'

'So I'm frugal,' she said lightly. 'Not all of us have deep pockets, Lex. You know I'm not in your league.'

'I also know that parting with a month's worth of high-end rent—unnecessary as it would be—shouldn't really bother you.' Lex's gaze had sharpened; his interest had been piqued. 'Sienna, are you in financial trouble? Is that why the sudden push to become a PA?'

'No! And no. Of course not.' She sent him a bright smile, but she couldn't hold his gaze. She opted instead for staring out the window at Sydney's suburbia. Subterfuge never had been her strong point. She didn't have to see Lex's diamond hard gaze to know that it was boring into her. She could feel it. 'There simply aren't that many advancement opportunities for art curators at the moment, that's all. I figure if I can combine business skills with my knowledge of the art world I might be able to pick up a PA position with a collector or gallery owner. Broaden my horizons.' Find some missing paintings… 'I will confess that a bigger pay cheque would also be most welcome.'

'So you *do* need money,' he said next. 'I knew it. I knew there was something to all of this that you weren't telling me. How much?'

'I *said* my money situation was *fine*. Just fine.'

'I swear you're the worst liar I know,' he muttered, and lapsed into a brooding, simmering silence. Lex didn't know the true extent of her woeful financial circumstances, none of the Wentworth family did, and Sienna took great pains to keep it that way. They'd given her refuge and protection as a child and friendship and family closeness as she'd grown older, but there were some things that Sienna didn't share with anyone. The small matter of her rapidly dwindling financial resources was one of them.

'What does it cost you to maintain that ridiculous mausoleum your mother left you?' demanded Lex suddenly. He didn't wait for an answer, he saw it in the dismayed glance she sent him because he cursed and his expression turned even grimmer. 'If it's draining you of every cent you have, *sell* it. Realise some profit or cut your losses, but get rid of it.'

'No.' There was no defending her emotional attachment to the old summer house set high on the cliffs of southern Cornwall. She didn't even try. 'Are we *done* with the commerce lecture yet?'

'You are *impossible* to help,' he said from between gritted teeth. 'Why can't you just tell me what you need like any normal person?'

'I have!' Sienna glanced over at him again, nothing more than a fleeting stab of desperation and pain, but it might as well have been a sword because it certainly made Lex bleed. 'I need to learn how to be a good personal assistant and you're going to teach me. That's all I want from you. That's all I need. Don't value add.'

'Dammit, Sienna!' Didn't she understand yet that that was what he did? 'I'm asking you one simple question. How much money do you need?'

'You don't understand,' she said quietly.

'The hell I don't!' Lex turned to stare out the window at the passing suburbs, cursing Sienna's long-dead mother for willing her a keepsake she couldn't keep, cursing himself for not figuring it out sooner. He knew Sienna was touchy when it came to money, knew he shouldn't have pushed her for answers she wasn't prepared to give, but, dammit, why couldn't she just confide in him the way she used to?

It wasn't until the limousine pulled into the circular driveway and stopped at the entrance to his sprawling luxury mansion that Lex made a determined effort to shake his black mood and play the host. He didn't bother pointing out again that it would be far cheaper for Sienna to live here with him than find somewhere else to stay. She knew that already.

The front door opened and Lex felt his lips curve ever so slightly as the dour and imposing Rudy stepped out. Rudy was doing his bodyguard-butler impersonation today—black trousers, a black T-shirt that strained across his massive torso, black wrap-around sunglasses, and an almighty scowl.

Sienna had seen him too. 'Rudy the territorial?' she queried with a glance that held equal parts wariness and apology.

'Yes.'

'You didn't tell me he looked like Steven Seagal.'

'That's because he doesn't.'

'Does he talk like Steven Seagal too?'

'Steven Seagal doesn't *talk*,' said Lex. 'His skills lie elsewhere. Come to think of it, Rudy doesn't talk either, unless he has to.'

'I swear you make some of the strangest decisions when it comes to choosing hired help,' she said.

'So I'm noticing,' he said and stifled a smile as her chin rose defiantly and those remarkable eyes narrowed in silent warning. 'Come on, I'll introduce you.'

Rudy nodded curtly in greeting as they got out of the car, then he headed for their luggage. Sienna followed.

'Sienna, this is Rudy. Rudy, this is Sienna Raleigh, my new PA. Sienna's a little different from my old PAs. She's practically family.'

Rudy's sunglasses zoned in on Sienna first and then Lex. What he thought was anyone's guess. The limo driver began unloading bags from the boot and setting them on the steps. Rudy joined in. Sienna went to retrieve the smaller of her two suitcases only to have Rudy swipe it at the last minute and set it firmly behind him. 'What's she doing?' he asked Lex gruffly.

'Hard to say,' said Lex. 'Sometimes she goes looking for an argument.'

'She picks up that suitcase and she'll get one,' muttered Rudy. 'Inside. Now. There's iced tea, chicken and cucumber sandwiches, and crème brûlée waiting for you in the west-wing drawing room.' The sunglasses zeroed in on Sienna again. 'You eat the crème brûlée last.'

'I knew that,' she said loftily.

'Family, you said,' said Rudy darkly.

'I've known her since she was five,' said Lex.

'Six,' said Sienna.

'And you employed her.'

'Believe me, point taken.'

Sienna stared from Lex to Rudy in indignation. 'What is this? Some kind of boys' own shorthand?'

'Did I mention the handmade French chocolates?' said Rudy pointedly.

'Nice try,' she said. 'But I'm more of an ice-cream person. Now if you'd said you had handmade triple-cream French Vanilla ice cream waiting for me in the west-wing drawing room I'd be there already.'

'There's one in every family,' muttered Rudy.

'I know,' said Sienna agreeably. 'Annoying, isn't it?' She looked up at the house, her expression faintly wistful. 'Thing is, Rudy, I'm not family and I may not be staying here so could you leave my bags by the door?'

Rudy ignored Sienna and looked to Lex. 'She's not staying?' he queried ominously. 'I've laid in provisions for two.'

'Family spat,' said Lex. 'I'll handle it.'

Rudy glanced towards Sienna, who'd abandoned the conversation in favour of making her way towards the front door. 'Does she sail?'

'Like a champion.' Lex had seen to that part of her education himself.

'Her bags will be in her room,' said Rudy. 'I hate clutter at the front door.'

'Don't mind me,' called Sienna. 'I'm moving through the front door and into the beyond. No clutter here. Come to mention it, there's *nothing* here but space and sunshine. What happened to all the furniture? Where's the umbrella stand? The sideboard and the vase full of flowers?'

'It's all right,' said Lex reassuringly. 'She's not serious.'

'You need sleep,' muttered Rudy. 'You're becoming delusional.'

This was a distinct possibility. He'd packed too much work and far too much wanting of Sienna into this day already. It was time to set things back on track.

He caught up with Sienna in the atrium, just inside the doorway looking curious and tentative all at once. 'What do you think of it?' he asked her casually, trying hard to pretend that it didn't matter what she thought. The house was a modern-day masterpiece, all sleek lines and open spaces. Lex hadn't designed it, the previous owners had, but it suited him well and Rudy kept it immaculate. Sienna would like it, he knew she would. She just had to give it a chance.

'It's lovely. Very private. Bigger than I expected.'

'I told you there was plenty of room. South wing's yours,' he said and, heading left, proceeded to show her the guest wing, complete with luxury spa, sitting room, breakfast nook, and four bedrooms. 'Take your pick,' he said. 'It's all guest accommodation.'

He led her downstairs next, to the pool area and gym, tennis court, boat shed, boat ramp, and dock.

'Yours?' she said, glancing towards the yacht moored at the end of the dock, and Lex nodded.

'Sienna meet *Mercy Jane*. There's also a speedboat called *Angelina* in the boat shed for getting places in a hurry,' he told her. 'Rudy maintains both boats and, when I say maintain, I mean he's fanatical about their function and their finish.'

'So…no getting to know the girls,' she said.

'Wrong. Befriend the girls by all means. Just cut your nails, take all your jewellery off first and don't lead them astray. Should you want to go somewhere and should Rudy decide that you're suitably attired, he'll have the speedboat in the water before you can say wouldn't it be easier to take the Porsche.'

'How protective is Rudy of the Porsche?'

'You can have a set of keys to the Porsche,' he told her with a grin. 'Rudy doesn't give a fig about the Porsche.'

He took her back upstairs and showed her the middle section of the house next, otherwise known as the west wing. 'Kitchen,' he said, and opened the door onto a spotless stainless-steel wonder. 'Library,' he said next, and showed her a room containing dark leather lounges, the odd desk or four, and floor-to-ceiling bookcases covering three walls. 'The billiards room,' he said, opening another door and affording Sienna a brief glance of yet another manly entertainment area.

'Is Rudy precious about his felt?' she asked him sweetly.

'You have no idea.' He ushered her through to the

formal dining area with its floor-to-ceiling windows and multimillion dollar view of the harbour, the bridge, and the skyscrapers of the city proper. Adjacent to that was the west-wing drawing room where Rudy had set out the food. This room had been furnished with comfort in mind rather than to impress, even though it boasted floor-to-ceiling windows and that panoramic harbour view. There was more in it, for starters. Deep, comfortable chairs, a settee for lounging on, footrests and reading lamps, table and chairs for two, a couple of sideboards…

'Nice,' said Sienna, wistfully eyeing the food. 'Where's the business hub?'

'Third floor. The staircase to the left of the atrium just inside the front door will take you straight there.'

Sienna nodded. Inched her way a little closer to the food. 'Where do you sleep?'

'Same floor as this, north wing.' Lex beat her to the food, poured two glasses of iced tea and handed her one. He picked up a chicken and cucumber sandwich triangle—no crusts—and ate it in a couple of bites before washing it down with tea. He had another, then another, then reached for a chocolate with a pistachio nestling on top of it. Would she stay? Would he be able to keep their relationship platonic if she did stay?

He didn't know.

He still wanted to protect her. Some things never changed. He wanted her to confide in him so that he could fix whatever financial difficulty she was in. She shouldn't have to give up the curator's position she loved for an all-hours job where she'd be constantly at some-one's beck and call, even if the pay *was* better. He couldn't stand the thought of it.

The only person whose beck and call he wanted her to be at, he realised grimly, was his.

'Rudy will ask you what you thought of the chocolate, you know,' he murmured. 'Try one.'

'You're trying to win me over with food,' she said.

'Not at all,' he replied, selecting a dark chocolate truffle and letting the taste of it explode in his mouth. 'These are *good*.'

He'd keep.

Sienna ignored the chocolate and reached for a sandwich instead. There was something very virtuous about selecting a chicken and cucumber sandwich in the face of crème brûlée and handmade chocolates. Besides, if she was going to stay here she needed to start building her resistance to items of extreme temptation. Like tempting truffles and ruthless rogues in sexy suits. She needed to start building it *now*.

'Rudy knows I'm not much of one for chocolate,' she said. 'He won't mind if I don't have any. I think it's good to come to an early understanding about such things, don't you?'

'Only if you're bent on declaring war.' Lex smiled in a way she was fast coming to learn was his ruthless pirate's smile. 'Rule number two for all successful personal assistants is to try and get on with the rest of the staff.'

'I'll do my best,' she murmured. 'What's rule number one?'

'Don't annoy the boss.'

Ah. Rule number one was the kicker. 'I'll work on that too. Speaking of which, when do you want to start work?'

'That depends on whether you still want to find alternative accommodation. If you do, then we'd better sort something out today.' He looked at her, his expression watchful, more old Lex than new. It didn't change her awareness of him one little bit, though. Her awareness was here to stay. All the appearance of the old Lex did was increase her confusion and add mightily to the overall appeal of the new. 'It's up to you, Sienna,' he said quietly. 'Nothing you don't want.'

Why-oh-why did he have to play the man of honour *now*? Why couldn't he have stayed the raider of hearts and made her decision on whether or not to stay here an easy one? Sienna looked at the food on tap and that glorious view. She thought of that fifty metre commute to work and the money she'd save by not having to pay rent. She thought of how blissfully *easy* life would be for the next month if only she and Lex could stick to work and friendship and forget all about the sexual curiosity kicking around between them. They'd managed friendship well enough for the past twenty years, hadn't they? They'd managed it without any romantic inclinations whatsoever, for the most part.

Nothing you don't want.

Well, she *didn't* want to become his latest conquest and that was that. Lex would honour her wishes in that regard; she knew he would. He was honouring them now.

'I'm prepared to give this place a chance,' she said awkwardly, and immediately wished she didn't sound quite so ungrateful. Lex was helping her out by taking her on as his PA. He didn't have to. He could afford to employ the best, but instead he'd agreed to train her, *and* he was paying her triple her old wage for the inconvenience. She tried again. 'You have a beautiful house, Lex, with an amazing guest wing and I appreciate the convenience. I'd like to stay.'

'Good.' Lex loaded up a plate with sandwiches, and topped up his tea. 'Get unpacked. Settle in. Go for a walk. Take a look around the bay. I want you in my office, ready to work, at two o'clock.'

'Yessir!'

Lex shot her a dark glance.

'Yessir, Mr Wentworth?'

'God give me strength,' he muttered.

'Well, what do your PAs usually call you?' she asked him.

'Lex.'

'I'll be there,' she said. 'Two o'clock sharp. Ready and willing to learn. You'll see.'

Sienna went straight to the south wing after Lex headed north with his plate of bounty in hand. She found her luggage in the largest bedroom and, mindful of rule number two, figured she might as well stay there. Rudy didn't do the full maid-service unpack of feminine fripperies—he'd simply placed the bags by the bed. Sienna made fast work of unpacking, considering her clothes as she went. None of the items she'd brought along were outlandish, but none of them could be classified as elegant professional secretary garb either. If clothes made the man—or at least reminded him what he was supposed to be doing—she needed to go shopping.

She found Rudy in the drawing room, clearing away the remains of the refreshments. 'You do good sandwiches,' she said by way of greeting.

'What about the chocolate?' he said.

'That was good too.'

His eyes narrowed. 'You didn't have any. No one mentions my sandwiches once they've eaten my chocolate.'

'Good point. Rudy, I have a problem. I need to shop.'

'For what?' he said gruffly.

'A business suit. Dark-rimmed glasses. Possibly sensible shoes, although I may not have the fortitude to carry through on that particular notion.'

He looked at the shoes she was wearing. 'It's a wonder you can walk at all.'

'The shoes are good,' she said. 'The shoes are fine. I've changed my mind about the shoes. But I still need a suit. Trousers maybe. No-nonsense shirts. Corporate body armour. Do you know of any shops nearby that sell that type of clothing?'

'Do I *look* like I frequent women's clothing stores to you?'

'No, but you might have a sister who'd know. Or a female friend who walks past a shop just like that every day on her way to work. You won't know until you ask.' Sienna smiled winningly and got a glower in reply.

'Don't you have other clothes you could wear?'

'Not if I want a constant visual and tactile reminder of the new corporate PA me—which I do. Today,' she added when Rudy grunted and headed for the door with plates and jug in hand. She scooped up the mugs, shoved a chocolate in her mouth and followed him to the kitchen. 'The chocolate is divine,' she said around a mouthful of it.

'Try chewing it next time.'

'I chewed it this time. C'mon, Rudy. I need some local knowledge. Are you sure you don't know anyone who dresses like Wonder Woman when she's not out saving the day?'

'Who?' he said.

'What about one who dresses like Clark Kent, mild-mannered reporter, before he morphs into Superman?'

He shook his head as if baffled.

'I need something to remind me that I'm working for Lex now and that I should just do the job he's paying me to do and not deliberately set out to annoy him,' she snapped. 'I want Lex to look at me and see an efficient personal assistant and not his old family friend Sienna. I need a suit! A no-nonsense, focus-on-the-job, don't-look-at-me-like-that *suit*.'

'Have you always been bonkers?' muttered Rudy. 'Or is this a recent development?'

Sienna smiled tightly. 'It's new.'

'I'll make one call,' he said. 'If that doesn't work you're on your own.'

The call did work, and within two minutes he'd arranged for some woman called Gracie Mae to collect her from the house in ten minutes' time and take her shopping.

'That's Grace to you,' he said curtly. 'She's the publicity officer for the Point Clarence Yacht Club, and mind you show her some respect.'

'You're a sweet man,' she said.

Rudy didn't even attempt a smile. 'You're so wrong.'

CHAPTER THREE

GRACIE MAE and her red BMW convertible pulled up to the steps where Sienna and Rudy stood waiting exactly ten minutes later. She was prompt—no doubt about that, but no one could ever say she dressed down. The woman was all Sophia Loren curves and sexy sophistication, with enough eye-catching jewellery on her person to stop traffic. She smiled languidly and blew Rudy a kiss before leaning over to open the door. 'One day you're going to take me sailing, big man.'

'Only if I lose my mind first.' Was Rudy actually *blushing*?

'I keep telling you there's no need to worry about losing your mind beforehand, sailor. You won't need it.' Gracie Mae turned that knowing smile on Sienna next. 'So,' she said, and gestured for Sienna to sit in the seat beside her. 'Rudy says you need a Wonder Woman costume.'

'I—what?' Sienna turned just in time to see the big man disappear inside. 'Rudy is confused. I need a business suit. Some dark-framed glasses. I need to look the epitome of corporate efficiency and control.'

'Even better. Because frankly, darling, the Wonder Woman look is getting old. You can call me Grace.'

'Sienna.'

'Beautiful,' said Grace approvingly as she drove out of the driveway and onto the road. 'It suits you. Been in Australia long?'

'Two hours.'

'And thinking about work already. I like that. Call me if you ever need a job.'

Sienna liked the woman already. Reaching for her handbag, she unzipped a side compartment and pulled out a pale blue airmail envelope, its folds not sharp and fresh but worn thin and ragged with age. She turned it over and studied the return address. 'Grace, may I ask if you know where Hornsby is? Is it nearby?'

'No, it's one of Sydney's outer northern suburbs. Right now we're skimming the outer eastern suburbs. Hornsby's about three quarters of an hour away by car.' Grace glanced her way. 'You need to go to Hornsby?'

'Not today,' said Sienna with a smile, carefully folding the letter with the precious address on it and tucking it back in her bag. 'I just wanted to know where it was. Is,' she corrected. I'll get there at some stage, but it doesn't have to be today. She'd waited twelve years…a few more days wouldn't hurt. 'Today I'm all about jet lag and business suits.'

'Business suits, business suits…I've seen some recently, but where?' Grace tapped thoughtfully on the steering wheel as they waited for traffic lights to turn green. 'Do you only need the actual suit or do you want the works?'

'The works. Except for the shoes. I already have the shoes.'

Grace glanced at Sienna's shoes. 'There's nothing

wrong with your shoes, don't get me wrong. They're perfectly acceptable. But I know where you'll find better.'

'Better is good,' said Sienna. 'Is better expensive?'

'Sweetpea, better is always expensive. Best tell me your budget and we'll work from there.'

'The budget is tight.' Lex hadn't been wrong about her financial situation. There'd been enough money left over after her parents' deaths for her to live modestly and acquire a fine education. But lately the costs of maintaining a crumbling manor house in Cornwall had got the better of her. The roof needed replacing, the wiring was a mess, and her savings were almost gone. Sienna needed to make money, not spend it. 'I need class on a shoestring.'

'Don't we all?' said Grace. 'But I know of a place where you'll find it. We'll go to Georgie's.'

'Georgie's is a boutique?'

'Oh, no, darling.' Grace shot her another one of those fabulous lazy smiles. 'Georgie is an artisan.'

For an artisan, Georgie lived in a fairly downmarket part of town by Sienna's reckoning, what with the graffiti and the neon lights and the men of disreputable intentions littering the street and all.

'Welcome to Darlinghurst, darling. Don't come here alone,' said Grace as she drove into a driveway and spoke into a security intercom set into the wall. Moments later the driveway gates swung inwards and they drove inside. Not a boutique, thought Sienna. A private residence.

'Do we need an appointment?'

'You just got one.' Grace slid from the car and headed for the door, her saunter as high-voltage sexy as the rest of her. 'Let's see what Georgie can do for you.'

Georgie was a remarkable-looking woman with a husky laugh, a penchant for neck scarves, and a dress sense that bordered on lush but suited her to perfection. She and Grace exchanged air kisses, continental-style, after which Georgie ushered them into a sunlit parlour with snow-white furnishings. 'And who have we here?' she said, turning towards Sienna with a warm smile.

'This is Sienna,' said Grace. 'Fresh off the plane from London.'

'Twirl for me,' Georgie told her. And in a hushed voice, 'If I had a face and a figure like that I'd be a millionaire twice over.'

'Working on it,' said Sienna.

'That's my girl,' said Georgie. 'Tell Georgie what you need.'

'I need a suit,' said Sienna readily. 'Maybe some dark-framed glasses. And shoes.'

A tape measure appeared as if from nowhere. 'Arms out,' ordered Georgie. 'Thirty-five perky—twenty-one flat—and thirty-six toned. Sweetcakes, you've got *curves*.'

'I'm aiming to cover them in a cloak of corporate respectability.'

'Girl's got style,' said Georgie and pointed Sienna towards a large Japanese-style screen in the corner of the room. 'You can slip off your clothes behind that while I go hunting. Can you do virginal, darling? Because I'm thinking white.'

'What?' said Sienna, poking her head around the screen.

'Perfect,' said Georgie. 'Back in a jiffy. Grace, will you have tea?'

Georgie disappeared, presumably to look for a business suit, possibly to make tea. Sienna ducked back behind the screen and slowly removed her shirt and skirt. Moments later two scraps of white lace and silk appeared over the top of the screen. Stockings followed. A white garter belt. Not a business suit in sight. 'Uh, Georgie? About that suit…'

'We start from the skin out around here, darling. Put them on and let's have a look at you.'

Sienna hesitated. She was in the market for a suit, not underwear. But the lace was exquisite, the garter belt matched, and lo and behold the lace at the top of the sheer skin-coloured stockings matched too. A girl could never have too many sets of matching underwear and stockings, right? A girl could at least have *one* set. She wriggled her way into them, fiddling with clasps and straps as she went before stepping tentatively out from behind the screen.

'There's the tiniest bit of support in the bra,' said Georgie to Grace. 'See the lift? Turn round, sweetie, and let us see you from the back.' Sienna turned. 'What do you think?' said Georgie. 'Are the panties too modest?'

'Borderline,' said Grace. 'That's what's so clever about them. Is that Chantilly lace?'

'Stunning, isn't it?' said Georgia.

'About that suit,' said Sienna and slipped behind the screen again.

'Keep the underwear on,' said Grace. 'Georgie has a holistic approach.'

As long as Georgie eventually coughed up a suit, Sienna was fine with whatever approach Georgie wanted to run with. 'I'm after something sexless,' she said. 'A disguise, if you will. Body armour. Easy on the va va voom.' She thought she'd been heard when the next thing that came over the top of the bamboo screen was a perfectly plain white cotton vest. Until she tried it on and the va va voom kicked in in spades. The neckline dipped and swooped across the curve of her breasts, framing them in sacrificial-lamb white. 'Is there a shirt to go with this?'

'Front and centre, Sienna dear,' said Grace. 'We won't know until we take a look.'

Sienna stepped out from behind the screen, lifting her arms to her neck and freeing her hair from beneath the collar. 'The hair will have to go up, of course,' said Georgie, coming at her with sewing pins and adjusting the seams and the darts to fit more snugly before crayoning in a new and even more revealing neckline for good measure.

'Uh, Georgie? I was thinking more along the lines of filling this neckline *in*.'

'Nonsense, darling.'

'I don't suppose you have a *mirror* handy?' said Sienna.

Grace shook her head.

'Not even a little one?'

A well-groomed, slimly built dark-haired man appeared with a loaded tea tray, greeting Grace with easy familiarity and sending Sienna a friendly smile completely lacking in sexual interest as he set the tray on the sideboard. Okay, so maybe she'd miscalculated. Maybe this get-up *was* frumpier than she thought.

'Raul makes the *best* tea,' said Georgie, still intent on reworking the neckline. 'He blends it himself. Raul, love, can you bring in the dove grey Armani from rack one room two?'

Raul nodded and headed for the door. Georgie finally crayoned in a neckline on the fabric that she was satisfied with and headed for the sideboard, pouring tea and handing it to Grace with a flourish before turning back to Sienna. 'No tea for you until we're done. The suit Raul's fetching is an elastine-wool blend with the *sweetest* little pinstripe running through it. It's very subtle but I think you could make it work.'

'I like subtle,' said Sienna. 'Subtle is good. And I'm really going to need something underneath this vest. I need to cover my assets, not flaunt them. A business shirt. With a collar. Buttons to the neck…'

'But, darling, *why*?' said Georgie. 'Why not showcase what you've got?'

'I'm having trouble settling into my new job—'

'She's Alex Wentworth's new PA,' murmured Grace.

'I want to be in control.'

'Trust me,' said Georgie. 'In this suit, you will be. What's your shoe size?'

'Seven.'

'Oh, the *envy*,' said Georgie, heading for the doorway. 'I take an eleven.'

Grace took a seat on the pristine white leather sofa, sipped her tea and smiled. 'How are we doing so far?'

'I'm not sure.' Sienna nibbled at the edge of her lip. 'I mean, I love it, don't get me wrong. But not for the office.'

Grace's smile widened. 'The suit will help. Armani never disappoints.'

Armani was a fiend, decided Sienna a few minutes later as she smoothed the suit into place. The fabric was gloriously soft to the touch with an elasticity to it that Sienna had never before associated with wool. The suit was subtle, the skirt modest in length, the jacket cleverly cut to emphasize the vest, the lingerie and the curves beneath without going overboard. This wasn't a clunky corporate disguise. It was sleek efficiency and understated sexuality and, boy, did it feel good. And then Georgie dangled a pair of steel-grey Italian-made stilettos with a three-inch heel over the top of the screen and Sienna's resolve to protest the sexuality of the outfit melted.

'Oh, my,' she murmured. Grace hadn't been kidding about the shoes. Sienna perched on the stool, slipped them on and stepped out from behind the screen only to have Georgie descend on her like a bee on a flower, straightening hems and pinning seams before finally standing back and pursing her lips. 'Slip these on,' she said, and handed her a pair of high-fashion dark-framed glasses. 'Now turn around while I put your hair up.' Sienna turned around obediently and Georgie wound Sienna's hair into a messy knot at the nape of her neck. 'That'll do for now. Now walk out to the next room and come back in as if your boss has just called you into a board meeting. Don't forget to knock first.'

Sienna knocked, but didn't wait for an imaginary invitation to enter. She just sashayed on in and stopped when she reached them, her hands on her hips. Georgie rolled her eyes. But then her sharp gaze roved over Sienna's snugly clad frame and she let out a very unladylike guffaw. 'Girl's got style,' she said. 'My work here is done.'

'It's gorgeous,' agreed Sienna. 'Divine. But I don't want gorgeous. I want sexless.'

'She's so young,' murmured Georgie. 'So misguided.'

'I know,' said Grace. 'Reminds me of myself thirty years ago.' She sent Sienna a rueful smile. 'Bear with me, gorgeous girl, while I dispense a little advice. I've dealt with men like Alex Wentworth for years. Smart, competitive, successful men. Used to getting what they want.

The sailing world is riddled with them. And what I've learned is that with those types of men, the best defence is a good offence. A successful businesswoman doesn't hide her sexuality behind some shapeless suit. She wears exactly the type of thing you're wearing now. She wears it with confidence and knows it for a weapon when she needs one.'

'Amen,' said Georgie. 'It's not about how the clothes look—it's about how they make you feel. How do you feel?'

'Powerful,' said Sienna. 'In control.'

'We rest our case,' said Georgie. 'I can have the alterations done and the outfit delivered to you by noon tomorrow. You just say the word.'

'I need a price before I say anything,' prompted Sienna.

'Oh, honey, you've got that businesslike attitude *nailed*.' Georgie laughed again and named a figure that would have kept a bottle-a-day drunkard in single-malt Scotch for a year. 'Listen to me,' said Georgie. 'I'm practically *giving* that suit away. The cost is in the lingerie and the shoes. I'm throwing in the glasses and my expertise for free.'

Sienna hesitated. Thought of the roof back in Cornwall that needed replacing. Thought of how long it had been since she'd bought new clothes.

'Fully tax-deductible, of course,' said Georgie. 'As are the dry-cleaning costs.'

Great. A suit that required maintenance. She could add it to the list.

'Think of it as an investment in your future,' said Grace.

There was that.

What to do? She really should resist. This get-up was so very wrong for a day at the office with Lex. And yet, perversely, she wondered what his reaction to it would be.

Sienna paced and preened while Grace and Georgie made small talk and left her to her thoughts. The shoes were going home with her, no question. So was the lingerie. As for the suit…

'I'll take the lot,' she said. 'Do you take Visa?'

Grace dropped Sienna back at Lex's mansion just on a quarter past one. Sienna waved her goodbye before trying the door handle, only to find the door locked. She buzzed the intercom with a chirpy SOS and then spoke into it for good measure. 'It's Sienna. I'm back.'

'The joy,' said Rudy's voice through the intercom, but he came and let her in and she beamed at him for his effort.

'No Wonder Woman outfit?' he said. 'Shame.'

'Grace and Georgie convinced me to trade up,' she said sweetly. 'The suit of destiny is being delivered tomorrow.'

Rudy stared at her impassively.

'You look tense,' she told him. 'You should have come shopping with us. Ironed out a few of those kinks. That or indulged in them. It's very therapeutic. Did you know that Grace has crewed in the Sydney to Hobart yacht race six times?'

'Yes.'

'And that she's got her hands on an Alliaura Supercat and wants to put it through its paces? Of course, for that she needs a crew. I told her to give you a call, what with one good turn deserving another and all that. The feeling is that you owe her.' Sienna made her way through the atrium and started down the corridor towards her room before stopping and turning back as if she'd just remembered something. 'When's your next day off?'

'Tomorrow,' said Rudy with a scowl.

'I must be a mind-reader.' Sienna's smile deepened. 'I told her that too.'

In the absence of The Suit, Sienna made do and changed into a lightweight skirt and a plain shirt before making her way up the stairs to the business centre at ten to two. Lex was already ensconced behind a glossy blackwood desk, a computer screen off to one side emitting a never-ending stream of stock prices, and another computer screen directly in front of him. He'd changed into different grey trousers and a white business shirt. He'd rolled up the shirtsleeves and left the top couple of buttons undone. If she looked in the top drawer of his desk she'd probably find a tie.

'Rudy said you went shopping,' he murmured, his gaze not leaving the screen, his fingers moving swiftly over the keyboard.

'Rudy was correct,' she replied, forgoing a chair in favour of perching on the edge of his desk. 'Where do I start?'

'With the Scorcellini bid. See if you can get Scorcellini Senior on the phone. Someone bought up three per cent of their stock in the time it took us to fly here. I want to know who. After that I need you to get hold of the last quarter's results for Zintex, Westshelf Mining, and Orion Transport.' He stopped typing and looked up at her, his gaze moving to her outfit as he leaned back in his chair. He took his time with the perusal, his eyes moving leisurely over her curves and turning her insides to mush before finally meeting her gaze. 'Rudy says you went shopping for a business suit.'

'That was the plan,' she said. 'All part of the new me.'

'So did you *get* a business suit?'

'Oh, yes. It's being delivered tomorrow. It needed a few alterations.' She sent him a smile. 'The new me was quite a revelation.'

'There's really nothing wrong with what you have on,' he said next. 'The skirt's a little short for the office, strictly speaking, possibly a little too bright, but your shirt is modest and blends in just fine. Those bone colours always blend. Team it with a pair of dark trousers and you'd have the perfect PA attire.'

'Really?' A smart man would notice a slight curtness in her voice, the tiniest narrowing of her gaze, but Lex didn't seem to. 'Something wrong with colour?'

'In fact,' he said, leaning back in his chair, a picture of dishevelled corporate elegance and power, 'why don't we keep the dress code around here modestly informal and I'll let you know in advance when I want you to don a suit? It's good that you have one, don't get me wrong. But you probably don't need to wear it all that often around here.'

'Don't mind me,' she said smoothly. 'I'm just experimenting with clothing that'll help me keep my mind on the job.'

'Good thinking,' he said. 'Rule three of successful personal assistanting the world over is to dress appropriately. In your case, given your very fine natural assets, I'd even advise toning down a little.'

'Toning down,' repeated Sienna, her voice deceptively pleasant. 'Really?'

'Just a little,' he said. 'You need to give your future employers a constant reminder that you're not available to them on anything but a professional level.'

'I see. You don't think that coming to an understanding about such things at the beginning of my employment would be enough?'

'Depends who's employing you.'

'Tell me something, Lex. Have you ever changed your workplace clothes in order to tone down the effect *you* might have on your employees?'

Lex smiled ever so slightly. 'No.'

'No.' It was okay for *him* to look distractingly fetching. She, on the other hand, had to blend. Grace was right. With men of his ilk the *only* defence was a good offence. 'Well, thanks for the wardrobe advice. I'll try and keep it in mind.'

'Your desk is over there. Yell if you can't find anything.' Lex eyed her warily, as if expecting her to bite. 'Was it something I said?'

'Why on earth would you think that?'

Lex's eyes narrowed and Sienna took it as her cue to get off his desk and on with her work. She was halfway to *her* desk—another beautifully polished blackwood confection accompanied by a black leather chair—when he spoke again.

'Sienna?'

'What?' He probably had another list of things for her to do. She probably should be sounding a little more obliging. She'd never had a problem with who exactly was in charge of any given workplace situation before. She was a hardworking, co-operative, non-confrontational employee, open to direction and ready to learn. At least, she hoped she was. 'Yes?'

'I've never seen you in a suit.'

'So?'

'I'm trying to imagine what you'll look like in one.'

Sienna thought of the suit of empowerment and smiled at the memory. Some memories were meant to be savoured. 'It's grey,' she said. 'The accompaniments are white. Nice, nondescript colours. I'm sure they'll blend in here just fine.'

Lex's eyes narrowed. 'What about the cut?'

Sienna smiled again, she couldn't help it. 'You'll like the cut,' she said. 'Armani never disappoints.'

Ten hours later, Sienna yawned and leaned back in her leather office chair, barely managing to focus on the computer screen in front of her. The evening meal had been and gone, exquisitely prepared and presented by Rudy the kitchen whiz. The ten p.m. snack Lex had insisted on was nothing but a distant memory. Midnight had come and gone; it was eighteen hours past her usual bedtime. Most normal people would have surrendered to tiredness by now, but the New York stock exchange had just opened for the day, Lex was still working at breakneck speed, and Sienna was attempting—unsuccessfully—to keep up with him.

'Got any money?' said Lex.

'Not any more,' she replied sleepily. 'Why?'

'The share market's moving. Give me ten thousand pounds now and by the end of the day's trading I'll give you back twelve.'

'Sounds wonderful,' she muttered. 'Use your money.'

'You want to stay awake, don't you? I guarantee that if we use your money rather than mine, you'll stay awake.'

'I don't want to stay awake.'

'Where's your sense of adventure?' he cajoled.

'I had a big day. I'm all out.'

'Okay, I'll accept five thousand,' he said.

Money. Always money. Maybe if she stopped trying to hoard what little she had left and started investing it instead, it might grow. It wasn't as if Lex was a novice when it came to working the stock markets. Maybe she'd learn something. Like how to turn a little bit of money into a whole lot more. Wouldn't that be handy? 'All right,' she grumbled. 'Five each. If I go down, so do you.'

His eyes took on a lazy gleam. 'I love equality. Pull up a chair.'

A minute later they were huddled around the computer screen and Lex had his money and hers riding on a hunch that zinc shares were on the up. 'What else is on the up?' she said.

'Energy and electricity,' he murmured and shot her a crooked grin with more than its share of lazy sizzle in it. 'Seriously.'

'Let's put five thousand each on that too,' she suggested. 'I spent a small fortune today on a suit I'm never going to wear. I need to recoup.'

'You spent *how much* on a suit you're never going to wear?'

'Okay, I *might* wear it. Never say never, right? I'm just a little hazy on the when.'

'Yes, but…*how much*?'

'What are those stock prices doing?' she said, trying to distract him.

'Dropping,' he said.

'What?'

'Look at you,' he said in admiration. 'Wide awake.'

'What does a good PA do when she wants to brain her boss with the hole punch?' she muttered.

'She resists.'

For that Sienna was going to need distance. And being cosied up next to Lex, elbow to elbow and knee to knee, simply didn't provide enough. Sienna pushed back her chair and stood up, smothering a yawn with her hand before stretching out the kinks in her back. 'You're on your own, rogue trader-san. I'm going to bed. Wake me in the morning if I'm rich.'

'And if you're not?'

'Hide the hole punch.'

CHAPTER FOUR

SIENNA made it to her bedroom, shimmied into her nightgown, crawled into bed, and slept hard for the rest of the night. Somewhere around sun-up she started to rouse, and toss and turn in the unfamiliar bed as her mind skipped backwards to another big bed in another lake-sized bedroom, and to the people that had populated it. Her mother, porcelain pale as she stared down at the shattered pieces of a broken vase. Her father roaring. Ranting.

'Stupid passionless bitch.'

Never mind that he'd been the one to throw the vase.

'Who are you to tell me what I can spend and where I can go? Who are you to tell me anything? Stupid crone.'

Sienna tossed and turned some more, needing sleep, not getting it. Her mother hadn't been a crone. Her mother had been beautiful, inside and out. Beautiful, and kind, and completely in love with the brooding, black-hearted bastard she'd married.

'You!' Sienna heard her father say savagely as she fell back into fitful slumber, only this time he hadn't been speaking to his wife. 'Get out. Out of my sight!' And as the drawing-room door had closed on her father's rage and her mother's frozen features, 'You're just like your mother.' A smile then, a smile just for Sienna. 'Pathetic, cowering, and weak.'

Sienna woke again at seven, startled into wakefulness when the bedside alarm buzzed into action. She certainly hadn't set it. Presumably Rudy the former frigate midshipman had.

'Man's got a death wish,' she muttered, groping for the clock and fiddling with its bits until it fell silent.

Not a good night's sleep, all told. Not one of her happier memories, although there were plenty worse. Plenty worse.

She contemplated rolling over and ignoring daylight completely in search of less fitful slumber, but if she did that Lex would doubtless come knocking and that would be bad. Lex was dangerous enough as it was; no need to hand him his ammunition on a plate. So it was legs over the side of the bed and a heave-ho as she hauled her protesting body upright. She pushed her hair from her face and finally coaxed her eyes open.

Ah, yes. The *other* lake-sized bedroom. The one she fully intended to exchange for a smaller model at some stage during the day. Sienna had become adept at avoiding her childhood memories. It was either that or be crushed beneath the weight of them.

If her more recent memory served her correctly—and it usually did—the en suite was approximately fifty metres away, somewhere to the south. Sienna got there eventually and took her time in the shower, emerging a whole lot cleaner and slightly more awake.

A hike to the cupboard garnered underwear, dark grey trousers, and a button up white cotton shirt. If Lex wanted her to dress down, Sienna would deliver. For a time. It would make the impact of the suit all the sweeter if she ever did decide to wear it.

Sienna dressed fast, accessorised with some pretty leather sandals and a dainty bead necklace in brown, black and beige, and figured that if she looked any more nondescript she'd disappear altogether. She power-walked back to the bathroom to apply a light dusting of make-up, and then hiked over to the bedroom door and along the never-ending hallway towards the kitchen. There would be absolutely no need for her to use the downstairs gym at any time during her stay, she decided happily. There was more than enough exercise to be had from traversing this house.

No one was in the kitchen, the vast dining room, or the drawing room. The library stood empty, so too did the billiards room. Sienna looked towards Lex's wing of the house but decided against going in search of him there. A man was entitled to his privacy. Someone—probably one of his former women—had once told her that he looked his absolute best between the sheets of a king-sized bed. Sienna didn't doubt it, but she didn't exactly want the image engraved on her brain either.

She went back to her room and collected her sunglasses and ventured downstairs with every intention of exploring the garden or maybe even heading out for a stroll. She hadn't asked what time Lex wanted to start work this morning—she'd simply assumed they'd start around nine like most normal office workers. Knowing Lex that probably wasn't the case. Lex had probably started work around six and was already in the hub wondering where she was.

Wrong.

Lex was swimming laps of the pool, his stroke smooth and powerful as he cut through the water with seemingly effortless ease. Sienna watched a little longer, wondering how she could have ever seen him as anything but the ruthless marauder he was. Smart. Sexy. Driven. Until yesterday she'd thought she was immune to him, but no. The rapid acceleration of her pulse at the sight of his sleek brown body suggested otherwise.

Sienna breathed deep, trying to push the attraction away, out of her body, out of her brain. She didn't want it, couldn't handle it. Couldn't handle him. Not if he really did decide to pursue her. Time to stop staring, and fretting, and go and explore the garden before Lex stopped swimming and Sienna started swooning.

The pool gate opened with a click and closed with a clatter, and Sienna strolled leisurely down to the jetty and along it, enjoying every bit of this peaceful, pretty spot amidst the chaos of a major city. Trust Lex to find it and own it. Trust him to know how to enjoy it.

The jetty rocked gently with the footfall of another and she turned and watched as Lex strode towards her, his hair all wet and mussed, a beach towel riding low on his hips and the rest of him splendidly naked.

Sienna couldn't remember the last time she'd seen Lex's near-naked self. Ten years ago? Longer? She'd called him scrawny once—she remembered that. It had been the day of his fifteenth birthday. He'd pushed her off the catamaran they'd been sailing and refused to let her back aboard until she'd flattered him half to death about the potential of his scrawny, yet surprisingly strong physique.

He wasn't scrawny now. Sienna stared at the stupendous example of raw masculine beauty heading her way—it was impossible not to. Lex's potential had been well and truly realised.

So much for not wanting an image of him without a whole lot of clothing taking up space in her mind. Because this one was here to stay.

'I like your sunglasses,' he murmured when he reached her. 'Although those lenses aren't nearly dark enough for you to be looking where you're looking.'

Oh. She dragged her gaze upwards past the washboard stomach and sculpted chest, over deliciously broad shoulders and finally found his face. 'My mistake,' she said. 'Nice towel. Great towel.'

He sent her a marauder's grin. 'How'd you sleep?'

'Like the dead.'

'How do you feel this morning?'

'Like the walking dead.' Sarcasm dispensed, Sienna considered the question. 'Not too bad, all things considered. Did I really buy ten thousand pounds' worth of shares last night?'

Lex's smile widened. 'You really did.'

Which meant that Lex had probably seen exactly how much money she had in her account. He'd been sitting right beside her—he had to have seen her meagre bottom line although he'd made no comment. He probably thought it was her working account. No need to mention that it was her only account. 'Do I still *have* ten thousand pounds' worth of shares?' she asked tentatively.

'No, you have eleven thousand seven hundred pounds in cash. We could have realised more but I bailed early and went to bed.'

'You're forgiven.' Hard to be cranky with a man who'd just made her seventeen hundred pounds richer.

'I hate to sound like a broken record,' he said, 'but you'd tell me if you were having money troubles, wouldn't you?' He sounded earnest. He looked earnest. Sienna adored him for his persistence even as she cursed him for it. But she wasn't about to tell him her money woes. If Lex knew of them he'd want to fix them for her and that was out of the question. The trick lay in making him *see* that helping her was out of the question. Sienna leaned her forearms against the jetty railing and stared down at the water, searching for the words that would make him understand. Finally, she thought she had them.

'The thing is, I can accept your helping to train me as a PA because I know that if you turned around tomorrow and wanted to become part of the art world I'd do the same for you. I can accept your hospitality because I can offer mine in return, albeit on a somewhat more modest scale. Maybe you can teach me more about this day-trading caper. Maybe that's an option I need to explore. But I won't take financial help from you, Lex. If I did we wouldn't be equals any more. And I need to be.'

Lex came to stand beside her elbow to elbow, only instead of leaning forward he leaned back against the railing and looked the other way. Once upon a time, Sienna might have leaned her shoulder into his and drawn comfort from that small contact, but not this time. Lex's touch no longer seemed comforting and familiar. It made her as nervous as a skittish kitten who'd never been touched. What would it feel like to be gentled by Alex? She didn't know. She wanted to know.

'If I needed five pounds and you had it in your pocket would you give it to me?' he said reflectively.

'Of course I would.' She knew where he was going

with this. 'If you asked it of me. But answer me this. If you knew there was a good chance that you'd never be able to repay me…would you ask me for it?'

'Sienna,' he began, and then stopped abruptly to run his hand through his hair before turning to glare at her.

'At last he walks a mile in my shoes,' she murmured.

'They pinch.'

'You lie,' she said. 'They fit you just fine. Which is why you won't be offering to take care of my financial worries any time soon.'

'I hate it when you're right,' he grumbled. 'Especially when it feels so wrong.'

Lex headed for the yacht and stepped lightly aboard her, before turning to offer Sienna a hand across, expecting her to follow. Which she did. His thumb at her wrist was warm and rich with sensual promise. Sienna's heart tripped and she let go of him fast. 'What happens if you fall in love with a rich man and marry him?' he muttered gruffly. 'I can tell you now that he'll want to take care of you financially.'

'Marriage isn't for everyone,' she said carefully. 'It's not for me.'

'I thought you might have grown out of that particular notion by now,' he said lightly.

'Nope.' Maybe she *had* been carrying the intention never to marry around since childhood, but it still seemed to fit her just fine.

'What about children?' he said next. 'You love kids. Don't you want any of your own?'

'Maybe.' Maybe there were certain flaws in her plan of no commitment. 'Maybe I'll have to just commandeer yours every now and again, and, anyway, I thought men like you liked your women free of commitments.'

'Not always,' he murmured.

Not a lot she could say to that reply. Maybe it was time to change the subject. 'May I come with you when you take *Mercy Jane* out next?'

'You may,' he said, his eyes lightening with the all too familiar promise of adventure. 'You have to see this city from the water. Preferably at dusk. Watch it come alight.'

She'd watched it come alight last night, from the windows of the work hub, and marvelled at its beauty. It would be even more spectacular on the water—Lex was right. 'Sounds wonderful.' It sounded downright romantic, actually. Which, given the way her body had reacted to his nearness this morning, wasn't such a good idea. Lex opened the hatch and disappeared below. Sienna made her way to the helm and started to admire all the nautical bells and whistles. 'I thought I had a lead on those missing paintings a while back,' she said idly. 'A pretty little pond scene turned up in a private collection, origin unknown. I really thought I'd found the Monet.'

'And?' Lex's voice floated up to her.

'It *was* a Monet. Just not my Monet. If I could just *find* it…'

Lex reappeared in the hatch staring up at her, his expression guarded. 'Then what? Then all your financial worries would magically disappear?'

'That's the plan.'

'Even if you do find the paintings, how are you going to prove that they're rightfully yours?' Lex said next, with irritating logic. 'The current owner might have the records to prove that they were purchased in complete good faith.'

'Not the Monet.' Sienna shook her head adamantly. 'The others, maybe, but the Monet was mine. It was a birthday gift from my mother. She even let me choose it from the catalogue. She would never have sold it without telling me.'

Lex eyed her steadily. 'But your father might have. He was perfectly capable of fencing those paintings and spending the change no matter who they belonged to.'

'I know,' she said quietly. 'But I think that if he'd fenced them or sold them outright, word of them would have surfaced by now. People would have seen them by now.' Two Picassos, a Rembrandt and a Monet—they were hardly insignificant doodles. 'If nothing else there would be innuendo about who had them. Rumours. Whispers.' And Sienna would have heard them. She hadn't chosen a career as a curator on a whim. She wasn't aiming to work as a PA for a wealthy collector on a whim either. If someone had those paintings squirrelled away, someone *somewhere* would know of them. It was simply a matter of moving in the right social circles and keeping her ears open. 'No, the more I look for them, the more I think that my mother put them somewhere. For safekeeping.' So that Sienna's father wouldn't do exactly what Lex had just suggested. 'She just…died before she could tell anyone where they were, that's all. One day, *one* day, I'll find them.'

'And when you do? What'll they give you that you don't already have? Wealth? There are other ways of acquiring wealth.'

'Not just wealth,' she said defensively.

'What, then? Happiness? Closure? What?'

When they'd been younger Lex had been as enthusiastic as her about going on a treasure hunt, but as he'd grown older his attitude towards the missing paintings had changed. He'd long since stopped seeing them as a challenging puzzle, and he'd *never* viewed them as a miracle cure-all. These days he considered her continued search for them nothing but a waste of time.

'Maybe closure,' she said quietly. Her mother's death. Her father's…indifference. Somewhere amongst all the venom and passion and sheer destructive force that had been her parents' relationship she still clung to the fragile belief that her mother in particular had had space in her heart for Sienna as well. 'Maybe I do see them as some sort of proof that my mother thought about me before she died. That she tried to provide for me. That she cared. About me.'

Lex sighed heavily, his hard-eyed gaze softening. He didn't say what she knew he was thinking. That if Sienna's mother had *really* cared for her she would never have taken her own life.

'Don't equate those paintings with your mother's love, Sienna. It's not healthy,' he said quietly. 'Mary loved you. Dearly. That's the way I remember it. Maybe that's the way you should remember it too.'

'I do.'

Sometimes.

'I just don't want to see you spend a lifetime searching for paintings you may never find,' he said. 'Maybe if you stopped looking back so hard you'd be more inclined to see those things that are right there in front of you.'

'Like what? A way to solve the current financial crisis I refuse to admit to having?' she countered. 'I'm on it. Reality has been dissected and rearranged with an eye to fiscal improvement. Why do you think I'm here? Which reminds me, what time do you want me to start work in the mornings?'

'Nine is fine. I usually start a few hours earlier to catch

the end of the day's share trading in the US but there's no reason for you to start then. I break at seven-thirty or so for breakfast and head back up to the hub at around nine. That's the general schedule.'

It was a punishing schedule by anyone's standards, particularly when he worked late into the night as well.

'Rudy normally serves breakfast in the drawing room,' continued Lex. 'This being his day off, he's prepared all our meals in advance and left them in the fridge. Each meal has its own shelf. According to Rudy you're to serve breakfast in the drawing room and clean up afterwards. Lunch is served in the drawing room as well and the clean-up procedure still applies. The evening meal is to be served at seven sharp in the dining room. Rudy trusts you know how to use a dishwasher and specifically told me to tell you not to mix meals.'

'Is that so?' she said airily.

'They're calorie balanced. Vitamin and mineral balanced too, for maximum uptake. Nutrition is another one of Rudy's little specialities.'

'The man's a genius,' she said. 'Of course, there is a school of thought that allows you to balance calories, vitamins, and minerals by the *day*. Which means you could, theoretically, choose food from all three shelves at every meal. Rudy would never know. Come to think of it, if I served the meals, *you'd* never know.'

'For some unknown reason Rudy took the time to write out the day's meal menu and leave it on my desk,' Lex told her with a grin. 'He's very thorough.'

'Isn't he just?' The cur. 'You do realise that I'm going to have to tweak *something* about those duties he left for me to do. It's an ownership thing.' Sienna didn't wait for

Lex's answer. 'Where would you like your breakfast served, Skipper? Out by the pool? Down here on the boat?' She sent him a conspiratorial smile. 'We could be really rebellious and eat breakfast in the kitchen. I'm good at that.'

'Rebellion?' he queried. 'So I'm noticing.'

'Eating meals in kitchens,' she corrected. 'From the fridge. You should try it some time, rich man. Take a walk on the wild side.'

Lex joined her on the bridge, his eyes telegraphing the promise of a very wild ride should she choose to take it. 'You think I don't walk on the wild side?'

'*I've* never seen it,' she said, moving aside to give him room to move and her room to breathe.

'Then you haven't been looking,' he murmured. 'Would you like to?'

'Eat breakfast in the kitchen? Yes. I'm all for it.'

'That's good.' His eyes had darkened. 'But it's not exactly wild behaviour, now, is it? Now, if I were to come up behind you and put one hand on the wheel and my other hand low on your stomach and pull you back towards me you'd probably find it unexpected,' he whispered against her ear as his movements mirrored his words. 'Hopefully you'd find it pleasant. But it's not wild behaviour. It's just normal behaviour.'

'Ah...Lex? Not for us.'

She didn't know which sensation affected her more, the heat of him at her back or the gentle pressure of his hand at her stomach. But together they set her aflame. Need warred with apprehension, both of them fierce, both of them demanding a response. The compromise was to close her eyes and stand very, very still.

'A man might breathe in the scent of the woman he held in his arms and put his lips to the skin on her neck, but that wouldn't be wild behaviour either,' he murmured as his lips brushed her ear.

Sienna gasped. There was no air left for breathing. Nothing but heat that threatened to engulf her. 'It wouldn't?' Because, as far as she was concerned, her body's reactions were getting very wild indeed.

'No. Not until you turned in my arms and put your hands to my chest and gave me your lips would things get out of control.' Sienna trembled in his arms, she couldn't help it, and Lex groaned and pressed her more firmly against him. 'I've been thinking about what happened between us yesterday, Sienna. I've been thinking about it a lot.'

'I'm surprised you found the time, what with your work schedule and all,' she said, trying to sound unaffected and failing miserably. All she could feel was Lex at her back and all she wanted was more.

'What can I say?' Amusement laced his voice. 'I'm a man who can multitask. I can also,' he said as his lips grazed her neck, 'recognise a problem when I see one coming. You and I, Sienna, have a problem. The only question is…what are we going to do about it?'

'I'm for ignoring it completely and hoping it'll go away,' she said fervently.

'You see, that's where we differ,' he murmured. 'I'm more inclined to find out how big our problem is. What say you, Sienna? You want to find out once and for all how wild this is likely to get?'

She really did.

She knew she shouldn't.

'Turn around,' he whispered.

Sienna turned around.

Hot colour rode high on Lex's cheeks as he stared down at her with eyes that held more than a hint of her own turmoil at the changes taking place in their relationship.

'You know what to do next,' he murmured.

Sienna started where Lex's towel left off, trailing her fingers over his stomach, ridiculously pleased when his breath seemed to catch in his throat and his stomach muscles clenched beneath her touch. His hands rested lightly on her hips, his feet were slightly parted, and she stepped in between them as her palms absorbed the pleasure to be found from tightly budded nipples amidst the damp tickle of chest hair. She lingered a while, learning the feel of him, delighting in the tremors that ripped through him. 'It's not so wild,' she whispered.

Lex covered her hand with his and guided her hand to the back of his neck. 'Yet,' he muttered and bent his head to hers.

Sienna didn't stop to think. She didn't want to think, just feel and taste and take. His lips were firm as she'd thought they'd be. Warm as she'd always known Lex to be. Gentle, as she knew he could be. Nothing she didn't want, but Sienna wanted more. He'd promised her wildness, he'd deliberately sown the seeds of her need for it. Sienna parted her lips and tasted him with her tongue, a leisurely slide along the join of his lips, a request for permission to enter. She expected consent but instead he pulled back.

'Be very sure,' he said gruffly. 'I'm not playing, Sienna.'

'Yes, you are,' she said, her gaze firmly fixed on his mouth, but right now she didn't care. 'You always do.'

'Not always,' he murmured, and set his lips to hers. They parted readily beneath his, soft, willing, following him effortlessly into a kiss that shattered his composure into a million tiny pieces. Lex had known need for a woman before. The sharp end of desire, the wanton side of willing. Known it and revelled in it, but nothing like this. Not like this. He slid his hands over the lush curve of her bottom, drawing her closer, needing her closer still. Sienna gasped and her arms came up to twine around his neck as she pressed against him and all the while her kisses destroyed him. Deep and drugging at first, until she pulled back for an open-mouthed exploration involving the barest brush of lips and tongue and an innate sensuality guaranteed to send him mad. He had her pinned against the ship's wheel with her thighs cradling him and her legs wrapped around his waist before she could do anything more than gasp. Another minute and he'd be carrying her down to the cabin and stripping her naked. Two seconds after that and he'd be buried inside her if he didn't slow this insanity down.

He broke free of her kiss, eyes closed as he fought for control. 'Don't move,' he muttered as she shifted slightly in his arms, framing his hardness even more snugly within the V of her legs. 'Sienna, please.'

She stilled immediately and Lex opened his eyes cautiously, only to close them again at the baffled mix of hurt and confusion in her eyes. He'd started this seduction, not her. And for all his considerable expertise in the area he didn't have the faintest idea how to finish it. 'I don't want to—' But that was a lie. 'I didn't mean to—' Also a fabrication. 'I'm not—

'Interested,' she said raggedly. 'For God's sake Alex, how many times do you think you need to say it? I get the point.'

She really didn't.

'Let me go,' she said, starting to pull away, all sharp elbows and panicked squirming. She was scared, he realised. Of him. 'I'm done with walking on the wild side.'

He released her reluctantly and watched her scramble across the deck and leap from the yacht to the jetty, her cheeks flushed and her eyes glittering suspiciously.

'I knew this was a bad idea. I *knew* it. Twenty years of friendship gone in a heartbeat and for what?' she said from the safety of the jetty. 'One stupid kiss! I valued our friendship, Alex. I needed it.' Tears threatened to spill from Sienna's eyes and Lex prayed they wouldn't fall. He'd rather slit his own throat than make her cry. She looked away, looked out over the harbour, and her chest heaved. 'Now what do we do?' she said brokenly. 'How are we supposed to get past this?'

'Sienna—' But she'd already turned away and started walking down the jetty towards the house. 'Sienna!' Louder this time. Sienna's steps faltered, but she didn't turn around. 'This wasn't some meaningless game of seduction, so if that's what you think you can stop it right now! I needed to touch you, needed to know what we'd be like together, and so did you.'

She still didn't turn around.

'Do you really think I'd throw twenty years of friendship away on a *whim*?'

Sienna's footsteps quickened.

'Goddammit, Sienna. *That was not a stupid kiss!*'

This time Sienna ran.

By the time Sienna reached her bedroom door and had shut it behind her she was breathing hard and heavy with the tears she wouldn't let fall. Panic had set in; fear of the passion Lex had conjured from her so effortlessly had mixed with an overwhelming sense of loss and the combination left her screaming inside. There had been no gain as far as she could see. Only loss, the loss of Lex who had been the one constant in a life full of loss, and she buckled beneath the weight of it. She put the heels of her hands to her eyes and leaned against the wall, striving for some semblance of calm, some interpretation of events that would help her find her way through this mess. Lex had touched her, invited her to kiss him, and she had. That had been her first mistake. Her second mistake had been in getting so caught up in Lex's kisses that she hadn't noticed that Lex hadn't been lost at all.

Lex had still been capable of coherent thought.

Lex, the supremely experienced seducer of women had reduced her to putty and then stopped. He'd had to ask *her* to stop. He'd stripped her down to her soul, but Lex had only been playing.

Footsteps sounded in the hallway. Not the loud clack of shoes on polished wooden floorboards, but the muted thud of a barefoot male. The thuds came closer and stopped at her door, replaced by impatient hammering. No prizes for guessing who it was.

'Go away, Alex.'

'No.' One word, quiet and implacable. 'Let me in.'

'Why? So you can kiss me senseless again just to see if you can make me want you and then stop? I don't think so. Once was enough.'

'I'm not going to kiss you senseless and stop,' he said tightly. 'I'm trying to repair the damage I've just done to the relationship I value above all others.'

'That's very sweet of you,' she said. 'Maybe later. I'm a little busy right now.' Busy trying to stem the flow of hurt from the gaping hole in her heart. 'Now go away.'

'For heaven's sake, Sienna, we were on a boat in broad daylight in full public view. Would you rather I *hadn't* stopped?'

'I'd rather you hadn't started,' she muttered darkly.

'You were just as curious as I was, Sienna.'

'Yes, well, consider my curiosity satisfied. Considering your ability to start and stop at will, I'm assuming your curiosity has been satisfied as well.'

'For the last time, I did not stop because I wanted to! Do you have *any* idea how hard it was to pull back from you? If we'd been anywhere else but on that deck we wouldn't be arguing right now, I'd be buried inside you!'

She didn't want to hear that. She did *not* want to hear that.

'You and I have a problem, Sienna. You *liked* being in my arms—you loved it. And I sure as hell intend to have you there more often. You're worried about ruining our friendship. You should be more worried about where this attraction is headed given what you already mean to me. This isn't a little problem, Sienna. It's goddamn huge.'

CHAPTER FIVE

HUGE.

That was one word to describe the workload Lex set himself and, by default, Sienna over the next four days. Exhausting was another word Sienna could have used if she'd had the energy for speech. She struggled to keep up, but she simply couldn't seem to stay alert come mid-afternoon no matter how many energy shakes Rudy set in front of her. By ten in the evening she was asleep on her feet. Rudy had begun to glower at Lex and make pointed remarks about bringing in additional help if the workload was set to continue on this way. Rudy had left the number for a temp agency on her desk. Sienna wasn't sure if he thought she needed to start looking for another job or if she was supposed to bring in help in order to do this one.

The tension between her and Lex wasn't getting any better. Something had to be done. Somehow, she had to make him see that working them both to death wasn't a particularly smart move when it came to finding a way through the wreckage their kisses had created. It was eight p.m. on a Thursday evening and Lex hadn't called it a night yet. Lex was gearing up for Thursday morning in London, but Sienna had had enough.

She shut down her computer, tidied her desk and shoved the to-do pile in her in-tray. Tomorrow would come around soon enough. She sauntered over to his desk and leaned her rear against the edge of it until she had his reluctant attention.

'I'm clocking off,' she told him sweetly. 'From now on I intend to work for you from nine till say, eight, on a daily basis, with an hour's break for lunch and another hour for dinner. I think that's more than reasonable. Anything over that you're on your own. If the work you want done doesn't get done in that time I suggest you employ additional help or find someone who *can* get everything you want done in a day done. Good luck with that.'

Lex sat back in his chair, his eyes narrowing. 'If you weren't coping you should have said something earlier.'

'I thought you might at some stage come to your senses.' Sienna smiled, sharp as a blade. 'But no. By the way, I'm heading out for a while. Don't wait up.'

He didn't like that.

'Oh, and Lex? You know that problem we had? The one where I had this irresistible urge to test your sexual prowess and find out what all the fuss was about?' Sienna leaned forward, in his face, deliberately confrontational. 'I'm over it.'

Sienna took refuge in the stainless steel wonder of a kitchen after that. It could have worked for her except that Rudy was still there.

'You want supper?' he said.

'No. And I have no idea what Lex wants so don't bother asking. I'm off duty. Possibly on strike. Depends who you talk to.'

'Took you long enough,' he said gruffly and Sienna looked up, startled. She hadn't been expecting support, but now that she had it she might as well take full advantage of the moment.

'Rudy, I need to explore your fridge. Possibly your freezer. Some people look to alcohol for fortitude and stress release, but not me. I need ice cream and I need it now.'

But Rudy was shaking his head. 'You'll need to go out for it. Do you good.'

He was absolutely right. 'Which way to the nearest ice-cream parlour?' There was a string of shops a mile or so back down the road; she remembered them from the drive from the airport. 'Out the driveway and turn right? Can I walk there?'

'Not on your own,' said Rudy.

'Can I take a ferry to somewhere with ice cream?' There was a ferry terminal not far from the house. She'd seen it from the jetty.

'No,' said a familiar voice from the doorway of the kitchen. Lex, looking tousle-haired and brooding and lethal enough to make a big jungle cat think twice about taking him on. 'Rudy, can you get *Angelina* ready? Sienna and I are heading out.'

Sienna ignored him completely. 'What about chocolate?' she said to Rudy. 'I've changed my mind about needing ice cream. Chocolate works just as well for millions of women the world over, right? I'm willing to give it another shot.'

Silently, Rudy removed a domed lid from a silver tray

sitting in the middle of the counter. A dozen perfectly presented milk chocolate truffles of varying darkness sat on a white paper doily. He left without another word. Probably to go and make ready with *Angelina*. Sienna leaned forward and eyed the truffles intently. She picked one up, nibbled at the edges. It was creamy and nicely textured, sure enough. But it wasn't cold.

'Face it,' said Lex. 'They're not your weakness.'

'Weakness can be cultivated,' she said curtly. As could resistance to grey-eyed workaholic bosses from hell. Sienna was living proof of it.

'I know this ice creamery on the edge of the water,' he said next. 'Forty-six different flavours. Rows and rows of toppings.'

'Only forty-six? How pedestrian.' She smiled at him none too sweetly for good measure. 'I'm not going anywhere with you, Lex. This evening's plan revolves around getting away from you. I happen to think it's an exceptionally good plan.'

'They make waffle cones on the spot as you order.'

Nice touch. 'What was that address again?' No reason why she couldn't find her own way there.

'Hard to say. I only know how to get there by boat. I could of course *show* you how to get there by boat.' He picked up a truffle and ate it with obvious enjoyment. 'They have a person sitting there making mini Bombe Alaskas. I hear they're superb.'

Bastard.

'C'mon, Sienna. I'm trying to make amends here,' he said.

'For working me so hard?'

'It was either that or haul you into my arms again. I

thought I was giving you time to get used to the idea of entering into a relationship with me.'

'What you were giving me was grief.'

He shrugged and sent her a crooked smile. 'Only a little.'

At least they were talking about the problem. She wanted to talk about it, Sienna realised belatedly. She badly wanted to understand what was going on in Lex's head. Why he'd chosen to set them on this course rather than stay on the one they'd been travelling along for years. She nibbled again at the chocolate. Sighed. Bombe Alaska it wasn't. 'I still don't understand how you can want me all of a sudden after a lifetime of never looking at me like that.'

'I looked,' he said. 'You just never saw me. You didn't want to see me.' He smiled grimly. 'You still don't.'

She couldn't deny it. Any time her thoughts about Lex had strayed from ones of friendship she'd slapped them down and kept them down. There was the small matter of self-preservation to consider. 'I know the kind of women you prefer, Alex. They're beautiful. Smart. Rich. You can have any woman you want. Why me?'

'You're beautiful. Smart too, except when it comes to relationships with the opposite sex. When it comes to those you're so scared of entering into the same sort of destructive relationship that your parents had that you'd rather not risk your heart at all. I've watched you, Sienna. No one gets close to you. You cut away anyone who tries. Even me. You're doing it now.'

He was right. She wouldn't wish the twisted love her parents had shared on her bitterest enemy. She didn't want it. Went to great lengths to protect herself from ever getting close to a relationship like that. Lex wasn't her father. He wasn't controlling, bitter, or malicious. But

Lex's power to make a woman incandescently happy one day and leave her weeping the next had shades of her father's behaviour in it. Too much of her father in it.

'Has it ever occurred to you that one of the reasons I don't want to get involved with you is that I've watched you play at relationships for years as well?' she said earnestly. 'You leave destruction in your wake, Alex. You walk away the minute you get bored, and the women you leave behind are devastated.'

'They're not that devastated,' he said. 'Most of them feel the loss of my money and the status that comes with it far more than they feel the loss of me.'

'Oh, Lex.' She shook her head. 'You don't seriously believe that?'

'Happens I do,' he said curtly. 'And might I just add that whenever you start mentioning *all* my women I start picturing a cast of thousands. There haven't been that many.'

'Oh, Lex.' She shook her head again. 'All right. Have it your way. I'll downgrade the number of women you've romanced to *plenty* but then I'm standing firm. You might recall that I've seen a fair few of them come and go.'

'And you might recall that you've known me for years. Average *plenty* out over that time and I bet I can get you down to *not excessive*. Okay, so I've enjoyed my share of female company. I don't deny it and I certainly don't regret it. Because here's the thing, Sienna. I've never entered into a relationship without the hope that I might find what I'm looking for. I've never left one while that hope was still there. Can you honestly say the same?'

She couldn't.

'You want to know why I kissed you?' he said with a twist of his lips. 'It's not because I'm some nefarious playboy intent on yet another conquest. It's because I've been looking for years now for a woman who understands me, fascinates me, and continues to fascinate me on every level. But none of them ever do. I keep circling back around. To you.'

Sienna watched in stunned silence as Lex ran a hand through his hair and glared at her for good measure.

'I have no promises for you, Sienna. You and I together might be the worst combination possible, and given your attitude to commitment it probably will be, but there's no other way through this for me. So here I am. Laying myself wide open and risking twenty years of friendship in the hope of forming a deeper relationship with you.' He looked away but not before Sienna had glimpsed a vulnerability she'd never seen in Lex before. 'You're not even going to let me in, are you?'

'Lex, I—I don't know.' She didn't want to. Self preservation screamed at her to tell him to stop this madness before it began, but this was Lex, and she couldn't bring herself to speak the words that would drive him away from her. She might not be able to give him everything he wanted from a relationship, but surely she could give him something? Enough to make him see that this woman he spoke of…this fascinating woman he kept circling back to simply didn't exist. There was only Sienna, and the Sienna she knew would never be able to hold a man like Lex, even if she wanted to. Which she didn't.

Maybe it *was* time to explore the attraction that pulsed between them. An affair with Lex would be passionate. Exhilarating, for a while. And then it would be over. Passion spent, minimal damage done, and if they were really lucky they might be able to salvage something by way of friendship at the end of it.

'Bombe Alaska, you said?' she said at last.

'Yes.' He glanced back at her and the sudden fierce hope in his eyes caught at her, dismayed her.

Pleased her.

'You'd better not be joking.'

'I never joke about ice cream,' he said solemnly. 'At least, not around you.'

To call *Angelina* a mere speedboat was to do her a grave injustice. Sienna didn't know boats the way Lex knew them, but she knew enough to realise that *Angelina* wasn't simply a ready means of transport for around the harbour. *Angelina* was a sleek and luxurious power ride, built for the specific purpose of giving whoever was at the helm a great deal of pleasure. Lex took his pleasure where he found it and always had, even as a boy. He took his pleasure now, skimming the beautiful craft across a smooth expanse of glistening water and leaving a trail of foaming whitewash in their wake.

She knew this man, his reckless smile and his quick-silver ways, his temper and his gentleness. Before too long she would know more of him. Lex wanted it. Curiosity demanded it. Her body willed it. She wanted her hands on him; she wanted his hands on her.

Knowing hands. A lover's hands.

Lex's hands.

Sienna had seen him at the helm of a boat many times before, but she saw him through different eyes tonight. His effortless command of the craft wasn't unusual—her reaction to it was. His innate sensuality had always been there—this time she allowed herself to respond to it, focus on it, revel in it.

'Call it a hint or call it a last-ditch effort to stop myself from turning this boat around and heading straight for the nearest bedroom,' he said huskily, 'but you'd see a lot more of the sights if you tried looking at them.'

The sights. Right. Sienna spared a glance for The Coathanger bridge and the Opera House. Very nice. But her gaze soon slid back to Lex's profile and then to those long tapered hands manoeuvring the craft so expertly through the water.

Lex sighed heavily. 'You're not paying the slightest attention to your surroundings,' he said and stepped away from the helm. 'And you think *I* have a short attention span. Here, you steer.'

It was no hardship taking a turn at the wheel of a craft like this. No hardship at all. Sienna even managed to turn her attention to her surroundings for a while now that she had to concentrate or risk driving them into the path of an oncoming ferry. That was until Lex gathered up her windblown hair and tucked it expertly under a cap, his fingertips brushing her neck before setting his hands to her shoulders.

'Better?' he whispered.

Sienna figured a whimper was as good as a yes.

'Turn to port, we're almost there.'

Definitely a good thing. She needed to be somewhere with noise. People. Alternative forms of temptation. Her attention was *bound* to be diverted once ice cream had been placed in her path, right?

Wrong.

For once in her life frozen dairy delights simply

couldn't compete, no matter how delicious. And it *was* delicious. Lex had to finish half of her Bombe Alaska for her, a tragedy of the highest order, except that somehow the combination of Lex and ice cream became temptation of the highest order instead. Lex's lips would be cool from the ice cream; his mouth would taste of it.

When Lex stopped walking to lean against a big wooden jetty post and finish off the last of her ice cream, Sienna left common sense behind and let temptation take hold. She stepped up close, took the ice cream dish from his unresisting hands and set it on top of the post before dropping her cap to the deck, and setting her lips to his.

Cool, just as she'd known they would be. Firm, just the way she wanted them to be. He shuddered when she ran her tongue along the seam of his lips, but he didn't pull back, not this time. This time he opened for her, twining his hands in her hair and taking her deep into uncharted territory. By the time she remembered where they were and broke the kiss, she was shaking hard and Lex was cursing, sailor fashion, his grey eyes signalling a fast-approaching storm.

'What the hell was that for?' he muttered.

'You were eating my ice cream,' she said defensively. 'What did you expect? Restraint?'

'A *warning* would have been nice. Or privacy. Definitely privacy.' He dumped the ice cream in a nearby bin while she retrieved her cap. She was setting it back on her head when he grabbed her hand, and headed for the boat, his long, purposeful strides forcing her to hustle to keep up with him.

'Where are we going?'

'My place. Your place. The workplace. Home. We're done with sightseeing.'

An independent woman might object to his high handedness. A feisty woman would remind him that he could at least *ask* her if she wanted to see more of the harbour before handing down declarations from on high. Sienna just looked at him and smiled a reckless smile.

'Here's the plan,' he said tightly once they'd boarded *Angelina*. 'You sit in that seat and you take in the sights. You do not move and you do not speak. You do not *look* at me until we reach the house. Are we clear on that?'

'Crystal,' she said.

Sienna became a creature of sensation on the way back to the hub. The wind on her face and the throbbing rumble of the engine as *Angelina* sped across the water. The rising tension coursing through her body on account of Lex's nearness and the realisation of where this was all heading. The lazy rhythm of the ocean's swell as they approached the outer harbour. The sudden loaded silence as Lex cut the throttle and steered the speedboat gently into place beside *Mercy Jane*.

It didn't take long to secure the boat. It didn't take long for Lex to walk her to her room. Once at the door he shoved his hands in his pockets and leaned against the wall. Watching. Waiting. Waiting for her to make the next move. But she didn't know how.

'Invite me in,' he murmured.

'It's your house.'

'It's your room.' His eyes were dark and promised heaven if only she would take a chance on him. 'I need to hear the words, Sienna. Invite me in.'

If she took this final irrevocable step towards intimacy there would be no going back to the easy friendship they'd once shared. When it finished, and it *would* finish, that would be the end. She made one last valiant effort to alter course, knowing in her soul that it was already too late, that this way lay heartache. She'd been stepping towards it ever since she'd first kissed him. 'We're friends.'

'Bonus,' he said.

'I'm your employee.'

'That definitely adds a little something,' he murmured.

'This is never going to work.'

'How do you know?' he said silkily. 'Until you try?'

Sienna fumbled for the door handle, turned it, and watched as the door opened silently. Tension clawed at her. Her body railed at her to forget her fear of failure and abandonment and to hurry.

'You know, this might come a lot easier for you if you just stopped *thinking* the moment through and just let it *happen*,' he murmured.

She took a deep breath and turned to face this man she knew so well in so many ways and not at all in others.

'When have I ever hurt you.' he said quietly, and clinched the deal, right there and then.

'Come in,' she said raggedly and held the door open for him.

She followed him in and shut the door behind her. She tried to smile but she was too nervous. She wasn't a virgin, but this was Lex and he made her feel like one. She took a breath and a step towards him. Another breath and he had her backed up against the door as he lowered his head and captured her lips with his.

He'd been expecting resistance, possibly token, possibly not. He'd expected hesitation, a physical manifestation of her earlier words. He didn't get any. What he got was warmth and softness and a quiet invitation to take a little more. He deepened the kiss and she let him. He trapped her between the wall and the circle of his arms and she let him do that too. And then she fisted her hand in his shirt and pulled him towards her as her kisses turned ravenous, instantly catapulting him into a world where nothing existed but blinding desire and the desperate need for more.

There was a bed here somewhere, Lex was sure of it, and he headed in the general direction of it amidst frantic kisses and the escalating need for flesh on flesh. She tugged his shirt free of his trousers and started in on the buttons, from the bottom up. He started on her shirt buttons from the top down. They tangled somewhere in the middle amidst laughter and curses and all the while her kisses fed his soul. Lex's shirt went, so did hers. He set his lips to her breasts the moment it was gone, demanding a response and getting one as she whimpered her pleasure and arched into teeth and tongue.

'Alex!' His name ended on a half-sob, raw and needy, equal parts command and surrender.

He lifted his head and met her gaze in wordless acknowledgement of a force far greater than the sum of its parts, and then he was unzipping her trousers and removing them along with her panties and Sienna was doing the same for him, her movements every bit as frenzied as his own. Sienna, with her quick smile and contrary ways. Sienna, who drove him mad and challenged his thoughts the way no one else could. Sienna, who made his body burn with a need so hot and fierce he could have rivalled the sun. Soft, so smooth and soft, as he slid one hand into her hair and the other hand down her body.

So damned responsive, the hand in her hair becoming a silken fist, part binding and part capitulation as he set his lips to her collarbone, her neck, the edge of her jaw…

Needing her abandoned response. Getting it.

'Alex, please!'

He wanted to please, he really did, but his body demanded instant gratification; no foreplay, none of his usual finesse. He wanted inside her, needed it more than he needed to breathe. This wasn't the casual recreational love-making of an adept; this was possession in its purest form.

He tumbled her down onto the bed in a tangle of arms and legs. Sienna's eyes were closed, the corner of her lower lip caught between her teeth, making the colour there flee. He wanted in, into her mouth, into her body before she drew blood; his blood or hers.

Lex got his wish; lips against lips, tongue against tongue as he sheathed himself deep inside her with a single smooth thrust.

One stroke, two, before Sienna's inner muscles began to contract around him, and then she was coming apart in his arms and he was following helplessly in her wake, feeding her abandon, revelling in it, matching it.

Enslaved by it.

CHAPTER SIX

SIENNA gulped down ragged breaths as her body recovered from its lightning trip to the stars. Lex was somewhere off to her left, sprawled on his back, his chest bellowing as he too struggled for breath amidst spasms of deliciously masculine laughter. Heaven only knew what he was laughing *at*. Wild monkey sex that had lasted less than two seconds, perhaps? The indelicacy of their current positions? The way he'd barely had to touch her for her to come apart in his arms?

All of the above?

'Here's the plan,' she said, her eyes tightly closed as she groped for a pillow to cover her face and hide her utter mortification at the speed of her surrender. 'If you take your shirt and your trousers and *leave* there's a slim chance I might be able to convince myself that this never happened.' Sienna hit softness with her palm and dragged the fluffy pillow across her eyes and her nose, leaving only her mouth free for talking. 'So….you know…don't let me keep you.'

More laughter from Lex and then movement from him. The mattress dipped but he didn't seem to be getting off the bed. No, it felt a whole lot as if he'd rolled over towards her and propped himself up on his elbow. Which meant that he was in all likelihood staring down at her—and there she was with her legs open and her limbs trembling, stark naked, in the lamplight. Oh, dear God!

Forget her face, the pillow was needed elsewhere. Breasts, no! Lower. No. Lengthways to cover both those areas. Sienna positioned the pillow for maximum coverage, hugging it tight, her eyes still firmly closed in an increasingly futile attempt to deny reality.

'What are you *doing*?' said Lex as he removed the pillow from her clutching arms, never mind her attempts to keep it.

Sienna eased one eye open and shut it again quickly at the sight of smooth supple skin encasing perfectly sculpted muscle. 'Pretending I'm not here?' she ventured.

'Sienna, look at me,' he murmured and she opened her eyes to find him staring down at her with an intensity he usually reserved for billion-dollar deals. 'Don't you think it's a little late for that?'

'Not at all,' she said fervently. 'I'm willing to give it a whirl.' Anything to ease her embarrassment at the speed of her capitulation. 'I, ah…I'm sorry I rushed you.'

'It wasn't that rushed.'

'You lie.'

'All right,' he said. 'I concede that we may have been somewhat hasty. But that's easily rectified.' The gleam in his eyes turned wicked. 'Touch me.'

'Again?'

'You didn't really think we were finished here, did you?'

'I was really, really hoping we might be.'

'No, you weren't,' he whispered and proceeded to show her why.

* * *

Round one should have taken the edge off his hunger, thought Lex as he set his lips to Sienna's shoulder, her collarbone, the soft curve of her breast. Unfortunately, it hadn't. Sienna only had to touch him for his hunger to become insatiable. She only had to gasp and arch into his touch for need to overwhelm him.

When she rolled him onto his back and set her lips to his chest he nearly launched them both off the bed. When she trailed her fingers up his thigh and slid her mouth even further down his body Lex knew he had to do something before this lovemaking session went exactly the same way as the last. Not that fast and frantic didn't have its place, because clearly it did, but a man had his reputation to think about, not to mention the woman in his arms. A modicum of restraint wouldn't go astray. Civilised sex. Languid sex. Surely he could manage that?

Sienna's palm skated across his erection and her tongue touched the tip, and all thoughts of civilised behaviour came to a groaning halt. Lex shot out from beneath her, cursing, half laughing, as he rolled her over and pinned her face down against the bed, one hand on the small of her back as he half straddled her to stop her turning over and reaching for him again. Better, much better, as he slid her silky hair to one side and nipped the back of her neck. Sienna moaned and tried to turn around but he wasn't having that. There was the small matter of control. Lex had it. He was keeping it.

'Here's the new plan,' he whispered. 'Close your eyes, think of England, and we might just manage the minute-and-a-half mark this time.' Lex ran his hand up Sienna's spine to the base of her neck and back down again until he reached the delightful vicinity of her bottom. He took his time exploring the curve of her buttocks, the slenderness of her waist, her buttocks again, this time with the accompanying scrape of teeth. 'There's no rush. I'm not going anywhere.'

Sienna whimpered but it wasn't with pain. She bucked beneath Lex's ministrations but it wasn't to dislodge him. There was no later, not yet. There was only now. Digging her fists into the sheet, Sienna gave herself up to it.

'Relax,' he whispered while his hands and teeth raised goosebumps on her skin. The soft abrasiveness of the sheet beneath her cheek felt like sandpaper compared to Lex's mouth on the curve of her hip. Another whimper escaped her.

'Shh.' A long, languid stroke of her back with his hand. The rasp of his leg against hers. A kiss between her shoulder blades. He soothed her even as he drove her body higher.

And then he was rolling onto his back and taking Sienna with him, her bottom nestled against his hardness and her shoulder blades digging into his chest as he parted her legs and slid his hand possessively over her hips.

'Relax.'

But Sienna's body wouldn't let her.

He entered her around about the time he set his fingers to her centre. He slid his other arm around her waist at exactly the same time as he started to move. Controlling everything; every caress, every sensation until Sienna was almost blind with the need for release. 'Alex, please! I can't see you. I need to see you. Touch you.'

'Later.'

'Now!' Sienna strained in his arms, her nails digging

into his forearms. 'Let me turn around. Alex, please!' She was almost there, almost there…

'No.' His voice sounded husky, strained, his breath a warm caress that whispered through her hair. 'Close your eyes, Sienna. Close your eyes and feel.'

Sienna closed her eyes, cursing him for his control and her lack of it.

And then she slid her hand down his arm, past where his fingers pressed firmly against delicate flesh and on to where their bodies joined. Slickness and heat as Lex surged into her, his body tightening beneath her questing fingers.

'That wasn't quite what I meant,' he muttered unevenly.

'I know.' She'd thought to undo him but it was she who came undone, arching her back the better to take him deep inside her as she began to climax.

Moments later, Lex followed.

Lex bit back an oath as his body twitched and softened in the aftermath of ecstasy. He lay on the bed on his back, with Sienna next to him, also on her back—this time minus the pillow. He considered the lack of a pillow an improvement, of sorts. The baleful glare Sienna slanted his way wasn't an improvement at all.

'You *restrained* me,' she said accusingly.

'Only a little. It was supposed to slow things down.'

'Well, it didn't!'

He'd noticed. Lex hoped he didn't look smug. He certainly felt smug. The passion and abandon Sienna had brought to their lovemaking made him feel like a king. Maybe a pirate king. 'Got any rope?'

Sienna's fist shot out and caught him in the gut.

'Oomph! Guess not.' Lex began to chuckle.

'Not funny, Alex.'

'Illuminating, though.' He reached down and entwined his fingers in hers in case she decided to thump him again.

'You asked me to touch you and then you *stopped* me. Again.'

'You can probably touch me *now*,' he offered. 'But I'm making no promises where future lovemaking is concerned. Every time you touch me I lose control.'

Sienna looked away and Lex discovered that he far preferred her glare.

'Say it,' he said. 'Whatever you're thinking, say it.'

'I don't know what to say,' she muttered. 'I don't know the rules of this game.'

'It's not a game.'

'I don't know the rules for one of those either. I'm working for you, living in your house, friends with you, and now I'm your lover. I've never had a relationship quite this complicated before.'

'It's not that complicated.'

'*You,*' she said with a tremulous smile, 'are a cock-eyed optimist.'

'I'm thinking that's just another term for visionary.'

'Fool,' she said, but her smile grew firmer. 'I need some rules, Lex. I need my own space and a way of knowing when you want me to be your PA, when it's okay to be your lover, and when you want me to just be your friend.'

Lex sighed and ran a hand through his already dishevelled hair. He'd known this would come. Sienna never had been one to stop analysing a situation long enough to simply go with it. 'All right, guidelines.' He didn't think it was quite the time to mention that he'd never been this neck-deep in complications before either. 'The main guideline being that the work gets done. There's no office politics to worry about because working for me is only a temporary arrangement and no need to be discreet because no one else is working with us. That takes care of our employee-employer relationship. As far as our platonic relationship is concerned it's business as usual. Any time you need your own space just tell me and I will do my utmost to make sure you get it. When it comes to lovemaking why don't you just consider me at your disposal for the foreseeable future?'

'You're very decisive,' she said.

'It's part of my charm.'

'There's no going back for us, is there?' she said a touch wistfully.

'No. But look on the bright side—and I really wish you would—I don't see why we can't happily mix business and friendship with pleasure.'

She sat up and glanced down at him, her eyes satisfyingly appreciative as her gaze swept over his body. 'I'm pretty sure the work will get done,' she said. 'It's not as if our lovemaking takes up a lot of time...'

Ow! 'Mind the ego, Sienna. Lucky for you it's healthy.' Alas, not that healthy. 'Was that a complaint?'

'Not at all.' Sienna reached for her clothes. 'Although...'

'Was it a challenge?'

'Would you like it to be?' Sienna's slow-burn smile sent a shaft of heat straight through him. 'A man like you needs to be challenged every now and then, don't you think? Keeps you humble.' Clothes in hand, she headed for the bathroom with a sensual sway to her stride that Lex heartily approved of. 'Now, if you don't mind, I think

I'll take a shower and get some sleep. My boss is a slave-driver, I have a huge day of work ahead of me tomorrow, and I need to be refreshed enough to get it done before I can go sailing with my lover tomorrow night.'

When the bathroom door closed firmly behind her, Lex sat up, his grin wide and his thoughts anything but humble as he reached for his trousers.

Sienna wanted more of him.

CHAPTER SEVEN

SIENNA worked her behind off for Lex the following day and together they cleared the backlog. She managed to hold the memories of their lovemaking at bay, concentrating on the work, sticking fast to the notion that the work had to be done before they could play. No touching, no distracting him, no undressing him with her eyes when he was watching, and above all no remembering the pleasure he could bring to her body.

And if the dampness and warmth between her legs was a constant reminder of Lex's possession and if her inner muscles rippled every so often in remembrance of him, well, she'd kept that to herself and turned her attention to counting ferries on the harbour instead.

At five past six Lex swivelled around in his desk chair and stole her breath away with a single look. 'Come sailing with me,' he said.

So here they were, as the sun set lower and the night crept in, taking turns at the wheel as they chased the wind in search of speed. *Mercy Jane* skimmed effortlessly through the water, responding obediently to Lex's every command, and he rewarded the little boat by making her fly. Sienna rewarded her own obedience to the demands of the day by slipping inside the circle of Lex's arms and letting the breeze caress her face as her body grew pliant and her need to undress him grew fast.

One ferry. Two ferries. Two ferries and a hydrofoil...

Sex with Lex had been breathtakingly good and she couldn't deny her need for more of it. No wonder his girlfriends wept when he left them. No wonder they begged and pleaded with him to stay. But he never had, he never did, and Sienna wasn't fool enough to think that this time would be any different. He saw, he conquered, he moved on. That was just his way. The trick to getting through these next few weeks would be to never take him seriously. Never give her heart to him so that when the ride ended she would remember it with joy.

So that when the ride ended she would not weep and she would not beg.

She could control this overwhelming need for more of him. She *could*.

'A good PA would do something about acquiring dinner,' she said, desperately trying to ignore her body's demands.

'A gentleman would have taken care of dinner reservations already,' he replied. 'A gentleman would have packed a picnic hamper and a bottle of champagne.'

'Gentlemanly behaviour is all well and good, don't get me wrong,' she murmured. 'But I'm woefully easy, I'm not dressed for dining out, and I know full well you didn't pack a picnic hamper. All I want is the champagne.'

'You'll find some in the fridge below.'

'Perfect.' Sienna looked towards the approaching inlet: a sheltered cove with a tiny strip of secluded beach. Five more minutes, she told herself firmly. Five more minutes and you can touch him some more.

'Sienna,' he said tensely, and the raw desire in his voice and the unmistakable hardness pressing against her left her in no doubt that she wasn't the only one practising restraint right now. 'Maybe you need to go and find that champagne now.'

'And maybe you need to find us a parking spot,' she muttered as she slipped from his arms and headed for the hatch.

By the time she'd found a couple of non-breakable champagne flutes and popped the bottle Lex had dropped anchor and joined her in the galley. 'How many glasses of this stuff do you think we'll need?' she said and quickly dropped her gaze when his eyes met hers, wickedly knowing.

'In order to replace an evening meal?' he said. 'A few.'

'How about in order to slow our lovemaking down?'

'A few.' His smile was pure rogue. 'Maybe we need to go back up on deck for a while and enjoy the sunset. Kick back and relax. Make small talk.'

'Small talk?' she murmured. Big ask given the shimmering promise that filled the air. But she made her way back up on deck and settled down port side, with her legs dangling over the side of the boat and her champagne flute beside her, and prepared to watch Sydney come alight. Raucous screams sounded in the distance, a cacophony of unexpected jungle sounds. 'What was *that*?'

'Monkeys. We're next to the zoo.'

'Oh.' Monkeys. Handy. No need to worry about the odd cry of ecstasy what with all those monkeys around. 'So…' she said. 'Come here often?'

He smiled crookedly and sat down beside her. 'Only if I'm in the area.'

She wanted to ask him who he came here with, but figured the list would likely be long, illustrious, and thoroughly demoralising. Small talk. Small talk… There wasn't a lot about Lex that she didn't already know. 'How's your mother?' she said.

The look Lex sent her was faintly incredulous.

'You said you wanted small talk,' she reminded him.

'Not about my *mother*. She's well, by the way. Says to remind you that you promised to visit her when you get back. She'll want to know how I treated you. She'll be hoping you'll say I treated you well.'

'Mothers and their expectations.'

'*I'll* be hoping you'll say I treated you well.'

'*I'll* be wishing I was paddling up the Amazon,' said Sienna dryly. Adriana Wentworth had served as a mother figure and confidante on many occasions. This would not be one of them. 'Maybe I'll go home by way of Dubai. Find another sheik in need of a PA. That could solve a multitude of problems. You'll probably be ready to move on by then. I may have come to my senses. There's probably no need to mention our current arrangement to your mother at all.'

'What makes you think I'll be ready to move on?' he said lazily, but his eyes were sharp. Lex at his most disarmingly dangerous.

'You always do.'

'That again,' he said.

'Face it, Alex. You enjoy women. And they enjoy you. It would take a rare woman who could get your undivided attention and keep it.'

'You're rare,' he said.

'Not that rare.'

'I don't know whether to be insulted on my behalf or

yours,' he muttered. 'Why can't you take me seriously, Sienna? What are you so afraid of?'

Of never measuring up. Of never being worthy of anyone's love. Of not being able to keep it. 'The usual,' she said finally, avoiding his gaze in favour of staring at the Harbour Bridge instead. 'You were right about me, Lex. I don't find it easy to let people in. Even you.'

'What are so you afraid I might find in there?'

Sienna picked up her glass, but didn't drink from it. Instead she played with it, cradling it loosely between both hands, her hands between her knees so that if the boat rocked and the champagne in the glass spilled it would fall into the water. 'Nothing you want,' she said quietly.

Alex fell silent at that and together they watched as the sun lost its battle for supremacy over the sky and moonlight took its place.

'Drink up,' he said finally and touched his glass to hers before draining his glass in one long swallow.

'What am I drinking to?'

'I'd say to us, but I'm not sure you'd raise your glass,' he said somewhat dryly. 'We could always drink to the prospect of long and languorous lovemaking.'

'So we could,' she said with the tiniest of smiles. 'Here.' She picked up the bottle and sloshed more bubbles into his glass. 'Have another.' Lex's smile grew lazy and intent and Sienna's pulse began to quicken. 'Cheers.' She finished hers for good measure.

'Sienna?' Even his husky murmur could set her to trembling these days.

'What?'

'Maybe you should have another one too.'

* * *

Lex's lovemaking had lost none of its intensity. Sienna expected passion and he gave it freely. She expected heat and he burned her up with it. But she hadn't expected tenderness and he gave her that too. She could feel it in the way he undressed her, and in the sweetness of his kisses. Lex wasn't just sating a fleeting hunger, he was laying himself wide open, revealing kiss by kiss all that he was.

Passionate. Gentle. Patient. Playful.

Sienna's first orgasm built slowly and lasted for ever.

There was nothing inside him she didn't want more of.

CHAPTER EIGHT

ON HER first free Saturday Sienna took the opportunity to escape the hub and head for Hornsby, by way of a ferry at first, followed by a train. From Hornsby station she continued on foot. She had a map and two good legs, it was a beautiful day, and she needed the exercise. Rudy's cooking was a little bit too good at times. Sienna was seriously contemplating having to become better acquainted with Lex's downstairs gym after all.

After twenty minutes spent walking in a south-easterly direction she found the street. Five minutes after that she found the house, a neat brick house with a red-tiled roof and a tiny, tidy garden filled with chrysanthemums.

She fumbled in her bag for the letter, wishing not for the first time that Elsie had included her phone number with her address. She'd tried looking in the phone book and ringing the directory, but there had been no E Blaylock listed at the address on the envelope. Then again, Elsie had left Sienna's mother's employment to go and look after her ageing sister. Maybe the phone number was in her sister's name.

Elsie Blaylock. Kind-eyed, grey-haired Elsie. She'd been housekeeper to Sienna's family for the first eleven years of Sienna's life. Closest thing to a grandmother Sienna had ever had.

Hesitantly, Sienna looked at the letter again. She'd found it last year amongst a box of bills and paperwork pertaining to the sale of her childhood home. Some twelve years ago now Elsie had given her address as 42 Aldersley Road, Hornsby, Sydney, Australia. This was the place. All she had to do was walk up that path to the door and knock, but still Sienna hesitated.

She should have written. Elsie would be in her seventies now, or thereabouts, and might not even remember Sienna. Calling on her in the hope of a clue to the painting's whereabouts was ridiculous. Calling on her because Sienna was desperate to sit and talk to someone else who'd borne witness to the travesty that was her parents' marriage was ridiculous too. And yet…

Maybe, just maybe, Elsie *would* remember her, and offer her tea, and start to reminisce. Elsie hadn't forgotten Sienna in the letter she'd written. It was a pleasant letter, a chatty letter that told of Elsie finding her sister's health much improved, and of her belongings finally arriving and of how hard it was to squash two lifetimes' worth of memorabilia into the one household. It spoke of scorching summer days and desert-dry gardens and a hope that all was well in Cornwall. Elsie's sister kept finches, Elsie had told Sienna's mother. Sweet-natured little birds with striking markings and a busy way about them. Elsie was growing quite fond of them but finches weren't children. You couldn't hug them. Elsie had asked about Sienna. Elsie had said that she missed the little girl terribly. Her last sentence directed Sienna's mother to give Sienna a big hug; a big bear hug from Elsie.

Sienna couldn't ever remember getting that hug.

Maybe, just maybe, she would get it now.

She opened the knee-high wooden gate and followed the path to the door. Taking a deep breath, she fisted her hand and knocked on the security door.

No one answered.

She knocked again.

And again.

Nothing.

She hadn't thought past getting here. She hadn't thought about what she would do if no one was home. Sighing, Sienna trudged back up the garden path towards the little gate. Maybe she could leave a note in the letter-box with her phone number on it.

'You're after Margaret?' said a light and friendly voice. A neighbour, studying her from the other side of the adjoining fence. A neighbour who looked to be about Sienna's age, with a lively, curious face.

'Er, no,' said Sienna. 'I'm looking for Elsie. Elsie Blaylock. This is the address I have for her, but I don't know…' Sienna shrugged and put the envelope carefully back in her handbag. 'The information is old.'

'I don't know that anyone named Elsie lives there,' said the neighbour, frowning. 'That's Maggie Cameron's place.'

Could Maggie Cameron be Elsie's sister? Possibly. Sienna had no idea of Elsie's sister's name. 'Do you know when Maggie might be back?'

The woman shook her head. 'No.'

'Do you know how long she's lived here?'

'Longer than me,' said the woman. 'And we've been here ten years. Do you want to leave a message with me for her?'

And say what? Hello, my name is Sienna Raleigh and

I'm trying to track down an old friend and a bunch of missing paintings? What if it wasn't Elsie's sister at all? 'No. I'll call back another time.' Maggie Cameron. Maggie Cameron. With any luck Maggie Cameron's phone number would be in the phone book and Sienna would be able to call the woman rather than turn up on her doorstep unannounced. Call her and explain.

Another week went by and Lex watched, unsurprised, as Sienna gradually worked the rhythms of his household around to her liking, taking to big business as if she were born to it and to Rudy as if it were her mission in life to annoy him. Lex didn't interfere because it was perfectly obvious that Rudy enjoyed her baiting and could more than hold his own. Rudy kept making triple cream vanilla ice cream and giving Sienna the tiniest taste before tasting it himself, deeming it highly unacceptable, and giving the rest of it to the next-door neighbour's Rottweiler.

When it came to their personal relationship Sienna seemed happy to spend her spare time with him, happy enough to share his bed or for him to share hers, but true intimacy with Sienna eluded him. He'd known that breaking down Sienna's barriers to intimacy wouldn't be easy. He'd been counting on their years of friendship to make it easier for her to trust him, easier for him to win her love, but when it came to love it seemed Sienna trusted nothing and no one. Whenever he tried to talk of a future beyond their time in Australia he repeatedly hit a wall so solid and so high that he didn't have the faintest idea how to climb it.

He didn't want to push. He knew he shouldn't push. Patience was the key.

Unfortunately, patience had been a little hard to come by of late. He'd turned to his work, knowing it for a distraction, nothing more than a convenient excuse to avoid focussing more strongly on what he wanted from Sienna.

Soon there would be a reckoning. Soon he would push for something Sienna did not want to give. But not yet. Not yet.

When it came to Sienna's work ethic, Lex couldn't fault her. Sienna learned fast, surpassing seasoned personal assistants with her appreciation for the nuances of negotiation and her ability to recognise what was important and what was pure ploy. If he hadn't had other plans for her he'd have offered her a permanent position and a pay rise by now, but he did have other plans so he kept his praise to a minimum. Sometimes, though, praise simply had to be given.

'You really were wasting your talents as an art curator,' he told her bluntly after she'd fielded yet another urgent phone call from Scorcellini Junior about Lex's latest bid.

Scorcellini Junior had a good head for business but he didn't have his father's experience and he didn't hold the majority stake in the business. Sienna had the younger man's measure. She also, thought Lex wryly, had Scorcellini Junior completely charmed. 'If they'd had any sense they'd have made you a museum director.'

'Flattery will get you everywhere,' she said with a smile.

'I meant it. You're good at this. See if you can set up a meeting with both Scorcellinis for Monday. The son is going to have to fall in line with his father's wishes on this one and the sooner he does, the better for everyone.'

'Your territory or theirs?'

'Mine. Wear your suit.'

'Er, Lex? You might want to rethink the suit strategy. You don't quite know what you're asking.' Sienna glanced towards the door as it began to open, her smile turning into an outright grin as a scowling Rudy stomped into the room.

'The quiche is cold,' said Rudy darkly. 'It was made to be eaten *hot*. When do you think you might get to it?'

'Blame Lex,' said Sienna the traitor, happily feeding him to the watchdog. 'I was good to break for lunch an hour and a half ago.'

'Blame Scorcellini Senior,' said Lex. 'He's had second thoughts about the opposing rescue bid. Seems we're back in the game.'

'I'm very happy for you,' said Rudy, in no way mollified. 'Perhaps if your personal assistant could let me know of any future schedule changes in *advance*?'

'Rudy, my sweet,' said Sienna, in no way cowed. 'The minute he *tells* me in advance, you will know.'

Rudy shook his head, clearly disappointed with Lex and Sienna both. 'I'll bring the lunch plates up.'

'I'll help you,' said Sienna, stretching her arms above her head before getting to her feet. 'What?' she said, at Rudy's offended look and Lex's amused one. 'I need a break. You need a break. Even Rudy needs a break. Look at him.'

Lex looked at him. 'What's wrong with him?' Apart from the scowl.

'How on earth is he going to make decent ice cream with a frown like that? Not that you need to keep trying,' Sienna told Rudy magnanimously. 'Grace is coming round at six-thirty this evening with a no-fail ice-cream recipe. We're going to commandeer the kitchen while she shows me how it's done.' Sienna gave Rudy her very best smile. 'Feel free to watch.'

Lex eyed the shaping battle appreciatively. Nice shot, straight over Rudy's bow.

'We might make use of the billiards room as well,' said Sienna. 'I hear Grace is quite the grifter. Apparently an old sailor taught her how to play when she was a child. Mind-boggling, really. Grace being so elegant and refined and pool being such a ballsy game. Wonder what she'll wear?'

Direct hit. Rudy turned and strode from the room without another word, with Sienna following in his wake, turning to wink at Lex as she left. 'We'll be right back with the food,' she said. 'You just keep right on working.

'Tell me, Rudy…' Sienna's voice floated back to him from the atrium. 'Do you play nine ball?'

Sienna followed Rudy into his kitchen, her thoughts only marginally taken up by the food Rudy had prepared for them, never mind how delicious it was guaranteed to be. Most of her thoughts these days were tied up with Lex. Lex's lovemaking, Lex's smile, his patience with her when it came to matters of the heart, and his ability to compartmentalise his life. The latter was really beginning to annoy her. Walk into that hub and Lex the lover became Lex the driven corporate raider. He did not push for any kind of physical intimacy at all within their working environment. Not even the brush of his hand against hers as he passed her some paperwork.

He could have given her *some* small physical contact, the rotter.

Because the only thing his noble restraint in that direction had done was make her want him more. Every time she went near the man her pulse raced and her body remembered the feel of his hands on her. Whenever he sat back and ran a hand through his hair as he stewed over figures that weren't to his liking she wanted to wrap herself around him and tell him not to worry, that wealth and the acquiring of it, although useful, were nowhere near as important as getting naked and making love to her.

Lex *knew* how to have fun. He and Sienna had had a lot of it over the years. But apart from when they were making love, he seemed to have lost the knack for it. He wasn't the carefree and impatient charmer she knew. The Lex of the past few days had been sombre and watchful to the point that she wondered what on earth was wrong with him. Maybe it was the Scorcellini bid. Maybe she'd simply never seen that part of him that could concentrate long and hard enough to see a difficult project through. Lex's companies made millions every year. He worked hard. She knew that already. But she hadn't realised that he had to work quite so hard to make it happen.

'Does Lex always work like a navvy?' she asked Rudy as she watched him load up two lunch trays with more delicacies than either she or Lex could possibly eat.

'No.'

Rudy the conversationalist. 'I mean, I know the Scorcellini bid is a big one, but Lex doesn't usually take all this work on himself, does he? He does have other employees who could do a lot of this work for him? Back in the London office?'

'Yes.'

'So why doesn't he let them?'

'If you ask me—and I really wish you wouldn't—he's making work for himself,' said Rudy reluctantly. 'A man usually does that when he's trying to avoid another far more difficult problem.' Rudy pinned her with a stern look. 'The way I read it, that problem is you.'

'You're right,' she said. 'I shouldn't have asked.'

But Rudy was on a roll. 'It seems to me that you're not deliberately messing with his mind. It seems to me that he wants something from you that you can't give. Normally he'd move on and source whatever it was he wanted from some other place. Given that what he wants this time might well be you and he can't actually get you anywhere else, he's probably feeling thwarted. He hates being thwarted.'

'Geez, Rudy. Can you go back to single-word sentences soon?'

'Yes.'

'Possibly not that soon,' she said, and Rudy sent her a long-suffering glance in reply. 'So, ah, given that your analysis is largely correct, what do you think I should do?'

'Simple. Either give him what he wants or leave. These trays are ready to go up.'

'Not simple,' she said darkly. 'What if what he wants wouldn't be good for him? What if he could do so much better?'

'I've always found him to be a very good judge of what's good for him,' said Rudy.

Sienna bit her lip.

'Have a little faith,' said Rudy gruffly. 'The man knows what he wants. Always has. Why not try giving it to him? Now about those trays…'

'Can you take Lex's up? I might take mine to my room. There's something I need to do.'

'Pack?'

'No.' Sienna smiled faintly. 'Not yet, anyway. I need to change clothes, that's all. And I have an idea.'

'Try and make it a good one' said Rudy.

Once in her bedroom Sienna nibbled at the food Rudy had prepared and hastily gathered together the items essential for her transformation. She reapplied her make-up and pulled her hair back into a sophisticated chignon before donning the corporate image, layer by increasingly gorgeous layer. The shoes came last and made her three inches taller and somehow a whole lot curvier. Jewellery she kept to the minimum—the Cartier watch Lex had given her on her twenty-first birthday; a pair of diamond earrings that had belonged to her mother. One last swipe of her lipstick and she was ready to go do business. She picked up the tray, grimacing at how much food was left on it, never mind that Rudy had overloaded it in the first place. Nerves never did leave a lot of room for appetite. Rudy would scowl at her. What was more he'd mean it.

Rudy was back in the kitchen, working on something floury, when Sienna took the tray back. He looked up as she carried it across to the counter and set it down. 'I wasn't as hungry as I thought,' she said somewhat defensively, but Rudy didn't even spare a glance for the tray. His eyes had widened fractionally; a muscle twitched in his jaw. He ran a floury hand across his mouth and Sienna was almost certain he was hiding a smile in there somewhere.

'What do you think of the suit Grace helped me buy?'

'I'm speechless,' he said.

'You usually are,' she reminded him. 'C'mon, Rudy, I need an opinion.'

'Where's the shirt?'

'The shirt was an optional extra we decided I didn't need. I invested in a vest instead.'

'Try wearing it.'

She pointed to the tiny strip of white showing just inside the suit lapels. 'I am.'

'Has your *employer* seen you in this suit yet?' asked Rudy. There was that smile again, only this time he didn't bother to hide it.

'Not yet. I'm just on my way up.'

Rudy nodded and began to clear the bench. 'Tell him I'm on my way *out*.'

Lex was on the phone, deep in conversation, when Sienna walked into the hub, but that didn't stop him from losing the power of speech entirely for a good thirty seconds. He swallowed hard, cleared his throat and forced himself to look away from the vision office fantasies were made of. 'About those terms…' But that was as far as he got for he made the fatal mistake of looking at Sienna again as she leaned over her desk and checked something on her computer. He closed his eyes and brought all his considerable will power into play as he forced his mind away from her hourglass figure and back to the call. 'Sorry, Stuart. Something's just come in that needs my attention, so I'll make it quick. You know I prefer to do business with you, but if you can't give me at *least* market rate I'll have to go elsewhere. Shave another half a percent off your lending rate, we have a deal.' He only half heard the other man's hasty reassurances that the lending rate was in fact negotiable. He'd never doubted it for a moment. 'Good. Fax it through. I'll get back to you. Fine.'

He swung around and put the phone in its cradle. Sienna had moved from her desk to her usual place, perched on the edge of his desk. Usually her sitting there while they prioritised the workload didn't bother him. The difference this time being that the little grey suit she was almost wearing did everything to emphasise her sexuality and nothing to cover it up.

'I thought you might want to take a look at my suit *before* the Scorcellinis came to visit,' she said with an easy smile. 'Just in case you figured it wasn't suitable.'

'It's…' Words failed him.

'Grey?' she supplied helpfully. 'Subtle?'

'Well, it's grey,' he said. Subtlety was a stretch. The skirt length was modest, true, but those shoes gave the outfit a whole new meaning. As for the cut of the jacket…

'It's comfortable too,' she said idly. 'And soft. Feel it. It's also very empowering.'

'So I see.' He reached out and ran a finger down the lapel of her jacket, deliberately skimming the skin where lapel met Sienna along the way. 'So I feel.' What the hell was she wearing beneath that jacket? Some sort of white linen corset? He didn't know but beneath the linen peeked snow-white lace. Office fantasies had never really been his thing. Until now. 'Take it off.'

'No, that would be stripping.'

'Okay, leave it on and *I'll* take it off for you,' he offered. 'No stripping required on your part at all.'

'Alas, I would still be naked. Where's the empowerment in that?'

'I'd probably be on my knees by the time you were naked,' he offered. Nothing but the truth.

'You're right. That does sound vaguely empowering,' she said with a slow smile that lit him through. 'I'll think about it. What else do you have for me this afternoon?'

'There's work to be done here somewhere.' He was sure of it. 'But it can wait. I think you need a demonstration of what you're likely to encounter if you ever wear that suit to work for anyone *else*.'

'Sounds taxing,' she murmured.

'I'll try and make it brief.'

'That *does* seem to be your forte.'

He took it on the chin. Nothing he didn't deserve. But he didn't intend to deserve the speedy tag a whole lot longer. 'About that suit…' he said with a smile that felt predatory and probably was.

'Gorgeous, isn't it?' she said artlessly. 'I couldn't resist.'

'You do realise what a suit of that nature will bring you in an office situation? Which is—by the way—nothing but trouble.' It was time for a demonstration. 'It'll start something like this. You'll be called into the boss's office and told to close the door behind you. There's your first warning.'

'I see. Thanks for the tip.'

'Sienna,' he said softly. 'Close the door.'

Slanting him a long glance, she slid from her perch on the edge of his desk, sauntered across to the door, and closed it. By the time she was done, Lex's mouth had gone dry and his body was harder than the Rock of Gibraltar. But he didn't rush things, not yet. The best seduction—just like the wooing of a torn and tender heart—required patience.

'The next thing that boss will do is use some vague and possibly work related excuse to bring you within arm's length,' he said mildly. 'You'll do it because you're used to doing what this man says. You'll wonder if this is about the work, you'll be beginning to think that it's not, but you'll want to give him the benefit of the doubt. Don't. Stay out of reach.'

'Got it,' she said, leaning back against the closed door with more than a hint of knowing challenge in her gaze.

'Sienna,' he said softly. 'My desk needs tidying.'

'So it does.' She walked towards him with a sway in her step that tested his self-control to the limit. 'If you could just move your chair a little to the left I'll do it now.'

Lex shifted his chair fractionally, and gestured towards the desk.

Sienna moved in, her legs brushing his as she bent over and began to tidy.

'That pile of quarterly reports, top right hand corner,' he said. 'They can go.'

Sienna had to lean far over his desk to reach them. It seemed only fair that he steady her with a hand to her behind, which, as fortune would have it, lined his thumb up exactly with the seam of her skirt. She gasped and looked back at him, her eyes several shades darker than they had been. 'Wouldn't want you to fall,' he murmured.

'Is this the part where I turn around and slap you?'

'Yes. Now is definitely the time. Use the hole punch. Cause a scene. Leave.' The skirt material was soft against his palm, the flesh beneath promised to be softer still. Lex forced himself to breathe, to wait, to think.

'What happens if I don't leave?' she asked.

'That would be seen as encouragement. You should avoid this at all costs.' Lex slid his hand lower and lifted it again to its original position bringing the material of her skirt with him, hiking it higher. She wore stockings. Suspenders. He couldn't see any panties. Lex bit back a groan.

'Where do you want these reports to go again?' she said huskily.

'Top left-hand corner.'

'I see.'

Lex needed to. He inched her skirt higher still, until her panties came into view, snowy white to match the suspenders and the stockings. Modestly cut. Demure enough to drive a man mad. He traced the edges, let his thumb skitter over her mound and felt her buttocks tense beneath his hand. He did it again and Sienna gasped.

'Could have been worse,' he murmured. 'It could have been my mouth.'

Sienna spun around about the same time Lex surged forward. He had her bottom on the desk and her legs wrapped around him at about the same time she grabbed his shirt and set her lips to his for a kiss that gave new meaning to the word wanton.

'I'm sure Grace said this suit would empower *me* rather than you,' she muttered between more of those wild kisses. 'Something's wrong here.'

'You're letting me take charge,' he muttered. 'You want to wear that suit and drive a man mad, you have to own it.'

'Believe me, I own it. But you're absolutely right. I'm working this all wrong.' Her thoughts didn't run to absolute domination. She didn't need a lot of control. Just some. 'Take a seat, Alex. The one you just vacated.' Sienna punctuated her statement by removing his hands from her and pushing him away.

Lex grinned and held his hands up in a gesture of surrender as he took a step back. 'Hot in here this afternoon,' he said conversationally. 'You'd be far more comfortable with that jacket *off*.'

'There you go again,' she said. 'Taking control.'

'Habit.'

'Sit.'

'Say please.'

'If you don't sit I'm afraid my suit will have to go back in the cupboard, never to be seen by you again,' she threatened sweetly. 'And that would be a shame.'

It seemed he agreed. He sat down in his executive chair, bold challenge in his eyes, every sinuous line of him a temptation. 'Now what?' he said in a voice that promised her whatever she damn well decided to take. A shiver of anticipation ran straight down her spine and into her loins.

'Now I straighten up your desk.' She did so, papers top left, hole punch on top of them, his telephone a fraction to the right, his computer screen a hue or two brighter. 'There.'

'I like my notepad slanted a little to the left,' he said.

'I'll keep that in mind.' Sienna turned back towards him, her fingers playing with the front button of her jacket, darkly pleased when his gaze followed the small motion and his expression turned intent. 'You're right. It is hot in here.'

Lex wisely kept his mouth shut as Sienna shrugged out of her jacket, lined the shoulders and the cuffs up, and folded it carefully before setting it on the edge of his desk. She leaned against his desk, as was her wont to do, with her hands either side of her and her fingers curling over the edge, and arched an eyebrow in silent query. 'You said there was work to be done. You usually have a list of things for me to do,' she prompted.

'I would if I could *think*,' he said huskily. 'But your vest has driven every last bit of blood from my brain.'

'You like?' she queried. 'I was a little unsure of it myself. I wanted a business shirt but they wouldn't give me one.'

'Have mine,' he said. 'Have it now.'

'Thank you. That's very sweet of you. But, no.'

'It's no trouble.' He had half the buttons undone already.

'Alex,' she said softly. 'Keep it.'

His fingers stilled. The buttons stayed undone, but he sat back in his chair, his eyes dark and hot. 'Now what?'

Sienna didn't know. Control was all well and good, but now that she had it she didn't quite know what to do with it.

'The thing about power,' he said silkily, 'is that you have to know how to wield it.'

'You're right.' Sienna regarded him wryly. This suit was proving more trouble than it was worth. And it was worth plenty. 'Thing is, I don't actually want power very often. Equality will do fine.'

'That again.'

'I know it's a stretch for you.'

'Only sometimes.' Lex's eyes narrowed. 'And might I just add in my defence that the only time I ever *have* dominated you, you liked it.'

True. Very true.

'Sienna—

'Shh. I almost had it.' The compromise of the century. Yes, there it was, all shiny and bright, but did she have the fortitude to go through with it?

'Lex, would you mind dropping by my desk some time this afternoon?' she said with what she hoped was an air of command. 'I have something for you.'

'I'll drop by now,' he said.

'Fine.'

Lex's lips twitched but he got up and headed for her desk. Sienna started walking towards it too, anticipation warring with a hefty dose of apprehension at what she was about to take. And what she would surrender.

'Take a seat,' she said. 'My chair will do.' It didn't have armrests like Lex's office chair. Armrests would be a hindrance to what she had in mind. She waited until he was comfortably settled before heading on over to straddle his legs, and ease her way onto his lap, her skirt riding high and her suspenders and panties in full view, should he eventually choose to look past her cleavage. Her body felt boneless, her skin hungered for his touch. Lex's eyes when they finally met hers held a passion and a promise guaranteed to drive them both to the edge of madness. 'You may put your hands back where you promised your mouth,' she said next.

He did as he was told, cupping her thighs so that his thumbs brushed the V between her legs. 'It wasn't a promise,' he said with a marauder's smile.

'It should have been.' She finished unbuttoning his shirt and pushed it from his shoulders, delighting in the silkiness of his skin and the hardness of the muscle beneath. She took a ragged breath and put her lips to his ear.

'Alex,' she ordered huskily. 'Dominate me.'

Alexander Wentworth the Third was not a man to take tasks lightly. He gave them his all. He paid attention to detail, to the little things that should not be forgotten. He liked to excel.

He started with the row of white buttons on her vest, taking it slow as he ordered Sienna to kiss him.

Lightly.

Tease me.

Sienna was very, very good at taking orders.

And then the vest went and Lex grinned wolfishly at the full impact of Sienna wearing delicate white lace and a smile just for him. The lingerie would have to go, of course, but for now he chose to work around it. The swell of her breasts demanded his attention; the swelling in his trousers demanded hers. The scrape of her nails along the hard ridge of his arousal. The scrape of his teeth along the lace at her breasts. An indrawn breath. A shuddering sigh.

It wasn't enough.

He wanted her on the desk so he carried her there, tenderness warring with his need to possess her.

Need won.

Dominate me.

He could play that game. There was no denying he knew how. But he didn't want subservience from Sienna and never had. He wanted her to argue with him when she thought he was wrong, chide him, fight with him, make peace with him.

He wanted her to love him.

'Hold all my calls,' he murmured as he sank to his knees in front of her. 'Tell them I'm busy. Tell them whatever the hell you want.' He parted her legs and pressed a kiss to her panties, right before he tugged them to one side with his fingers. 'Now, put your hands in my hair and keep them there.'

CHAPTER NINE

BY SIX o' clock that evening Sienna's desk was clear of everything, including her. She felt sated, dominated, and well pleased with the way the afternoon had progressed, but there was no escaping the fact that they'd neglected the work, or that as a result Lex's desk was currently overloaded with work that only he could do.

'You may as well go,' he said, looking back at his desk with the distracted expression Sienna had come to associate with calculations that contained far too many zeroes. 'I still need to finish up a few things here. Go make ice cream with Grace. Bring me up some later. Torture Rudy. Have fun.'

'You work too hard,' she said.

Lex smiled fleetingly and rubbed his temple. 'Only sometimes.'

'Only a lot.' Sienna perched on the edge of his desk and regarded him solemnly. 'Why don't you come down for a break around seven-thirty? We'll be in the billiards room by then, emasculating the felt.'

'Have you confirmed what Grace will be wearing?'

'No idea.'

'What will *you* be wearing?' murmured Lex, his eyes darkening as he scanned her suit.

'A smile.'

'Good choice,' he said. 'What else?'

'I haven't decided yet.'

The intercom cracked to life and Rudy's gruff voice filled the room. 'Grace is at the door,' he said. 'Who's letting her in?'

Sienna leaned over Lex's desk and pressed the intercom. 'Rudy, would you? I'm just finishing up here with Lex. I'll be down in a minute.'

'You're getting very good at giving orders,' Lex murmured as she broke the connection. His words were directed at her, she was sure of it. But his gaze was on the swell of her breasts, lovingly encased in virginal white and cloaked thereafter in the softest of grey.

'What can I say? I'm feeling very empowered.' Sienna grinned at his continued distraction and took a deep and undulating breath just because she could. 'Man, I love this suit.'

'You're also getting extremely good at manipulating events to your liking,' he muttered, finally lifting his gaze to hers.

'That's just natural aptitude. Is Rudy cooking tonight?'

Lex shook his head. 'It's his night off.'

'So if he could be persuaded to join Grace and I in the kitchen—as our guest—would that be a problem for you?'

'As in how strong a hold does the English class system have on you, Lex?'

Sienna nodded.

'Not that strong. Rudy's a good man. He cooks for me and looks after this place because it suits him. He maintains the distance between employer and employee because that suits him too. He knows he's welcome at my table; he's sat at it before. I've sat at his. Ask him to join you by all means. Just don't be surprised if he refuses. He's uncomfortable around women as a rule.'

'He's not uncomfortable around me.'

'That's because you're at war with him. Retaliation gives him something to do.'

'You're a good man, Alexander Wentworth the Third.' She leaned towards him and brushed his lips with hers. 'Work fast.'

He captured her lips again for a kiss that quickly turned hungry. He cursed and sat back in his chair looking pained. 'Sienna, I need another hour before I can finish up here. Or four.'

'I know.' Sienna sighed and dropped a kiss on his hair before heading for the door. 'Do your work. I can entertain myself. Come down when you can. I can wait.'

Barely.

Sienna's watch told her that Grace was ten minutes early. Her prolonged bout of afternoon lovemaking with Lex made freshening up before she met up with her guest a necessity. She would poke her head around the kitchen door and beg some time, she decided as she headed down the stairs and into the atrium. How much time depended on the vibe in the kitchen. It would also depend on not giving Rudy the opportunity to leave.

'Grace, I'm so glad you could come over,' she told the older woman when she reached the entrance to the kitchen, trying to decide whether half in the doorway and half out was better than mostly out or mostly in. Neither would hide her general state of dishevelment for long. Rudy stood on the fridge side of the kitchen counter and appeared to be pouring Grace a glass of champagne. Grace stood on the other side of the counter wearing a red chiffon shift with a plunging neckline, slimline navy trousers, and high-heeled pumps in the exact same blue as the trousers. 'Are you sure you're ready to make ice cream, though? You look much too elegant to do anything so mundane.'

'Gorgeous girl, I am wearing the perfect ice-cream-making attire,' countered Grace. 'Ice-cream making is a seriously glamorous endeavour. At least, it is when I do it. You, on the other hand, don't look dressed for cooking at all. You look like you've just walked in from a hard day at the office.' Grace's smile deepened. 'Nice to see the corporate image in play.'

'I'd like to take the corporate image out of play if you can give me a few minutes to change clothes and freshen up,' Sienna said hastily. 'Would you mind if I left you in Rudy's care a little longer?'

'Not at all,' said Grace, but that was only half the equation as far as Sienna was concerned.

'Rudy?'

'Go,' said Rudy gruffly.

'Darling man,' she said, and left before he could change his mind.

Sienna made it to her room with every intention of taking the fastest shower she'd ever had, followed by slipping into a casual shirt and pair of trousers, and thereafter returning immediately to the kitchen. But she remembered Lex's touch as she removed her suit and began to unclip her stockings. She remembered the appreciation he'd finally got around to showing for her lingerie and her hands paused as she let the memories take her over. Making love with Lex was like flying naked into the sun; a body burned hotter and brighter with every passing moment until heat finally ripped it apart. In that incandescent moment Sienna was his and only his. Nothing else existed. There was only Lex and her hunger for him. No one else's lovemaking had ever come close. She doubted anyone's ever would. He had her measure—body, soul, and mind. If she allowed it to, the thought of him could fill every last piece of her with longing.

Was this what it felt like to love?

Was this what her mother had felt for her father? Was that why she'd taken her life when their marriage had fallen apart?

Hadn't there been *any* love left over for anyone else?

'I would have had love left over,' she muttered as she came to her senses and continued to strip down to skin and head for the shower. 'I would have had love for my child no matter how badly that child's father had betrayed me. I wouldn't have let him have it all.'

She didn't intend to let Lex have it all now.

Did that make her less in love with Lex than her mother had been with her father?

Or more?

It was all too confusing. Trying to relate her feelings for Lex with what she knew of love from the example set by her parents was a guaranteed recipe for heartache. Far better to simply admit that she had no idea how a functioning adult relationship between two people who cared for each other worked and get on with the process of finding out.

Sienna soaped down fast, taking full advantage of the

calming scent of sandalwood and ginger that teased at her senses. Grace was waiting, Grace and Rudy, and there was no time for an out and out analysis of love right now. No time for memories, heartbreaking or otherwise.

Sienna never had been able to afford to live in the past. She didn't particularly want to think about the future. There was only the present.

'The secret to handling a man like Alex Wentworth,' said Grace as she sampled her ice-cream-making efforts and gave a nod of approval, 'is to keep him guessing.'

'No problem there, considering I have no idea what I want from him,' replied Sienna with a frankness born of French champagne on an empty stomach. 'Except the sex. I'm completely sold on that.'

Grace had brought the champagne along for the evening and insisted on it being an accompaniment to their ice-cream-making efforts. Sienna was currently contemplating the merits of adding Grace's ice cream to France's finest and turning it into a spider. Rudy was nowhere to be seen—he'd fled the minute Sienna had returned, which was probably for the best, decided Sienna. 'Rudy would die if he saw the mess we're making of his kitchen.'

'Rudy's not here,' said Grace. 'I swear it's enough to give a confident woman a complex. Did you know he designs ocean-going yachts? He's having one built now—eight point two million dollars' worth of clean lines and luxury specifications. I've seen the plans.'

'Who's financing it?'

'Rudy and Alex. Apparently they plan to venture into the yacht-building business together if this one's a success. I've seen a lot of boats in my time, Sienna. This one's a winner. I'd order one myself if I could afford to.' Grace's expression grew dreamy. 'A woman could do a lot worse than to sail the world on a boat like that with the right man at her side.'

'Is Rudy the right man?' queried Sienna and Grace smiled wryly.

'He could be. If I could just get past his shyness.'

There was that. 'The trick to handling a man like Rudy,' said Sienna, 'is to make him feel needed. Are you hungry? Because I'm starving.' She headed for the intercom and pressed the buzzer. 'Rudy, are you there?'

There was a brief pause followed by the crackle of static.

'No,' said Rudy's voice. The wit.

'Grace and I are thinking of ordering takeaway for dinner. We need guidance.'

'No, you need a phone.'

'Or we could throw a little something together ourselves. You don't mind if we use a few of the ingredients in the fridge, do you?' Grace crossed to the fridge, opened the door and began pulling out fixings. Sienna listed them as they landed on the counter. 'The prosciutto, the veal, the mascarpone…looks like we're going Italian. Grace wants to know if you're doing anything with the roasted pine nuts and pumpkin?'

'Out of my fridge,' he said curtly. '*I'll* cook the dinner.'

'Rudy has graciously offered to cook for us,' Sienna told Grace. 'Shall we accept?'

'He's such a gentleman,' replied Grace, shutting the fridge door and resuming her position propped against the counter. 'Of course we accept. But only if he lets us help with the preparation and clean up, and only if he helps us eat it.'

'Grace is going to be your able-bodied assistant and you are hereby officially invited to join us for dinner,' translated Sienna.

'I'll cook,' he said. 'That's all.'

'Sorry, Rudy. It's a package deal. You're either all in or you stay out of the kitchen. Grace wants to know if you're saving the kipfler potatoes for anything special. Hang on.' Sienna grinned at Grace, who had yet to even find the kipfler potatoes, let alone decide what to do with them. 'Grace wants to know if you have any pink sea salt.' Grace was sipping champagne and watching with dry amusement as Sienna banged a couple of pots down on the bench for chaotic effect. 'I don't suppose you have a little white apron she could use?'

Dead silence at that and Sienna wondered if she'd overplayed her hand.

'Tell her she does not need an apron.' Did Rudy's voice sound gruffer than usual? Hard to tell over the intercom. *'I will cook the meal.'*

'Perfect. See you soon. I'll make a start on the hors d'oeuvres, though, shall I? I'm thinking champagne spiders but I'm in a quandary.' Grace was laughing silently as Sienna closed in for the kill. 'One scoop or two?'

Fifteen minutes later the stainless-steel state-of-the-art kitchen had been restored to order and dinner was taking shape beneath Rudy's watchful gaze as he guardedly let Grace loose on his precious ingredients. He'd declined the champagne, with or without the addition of ice cream, but accepted a beer and even allowed Sienna to put some music on. She'd chosen a classic mix of American jazz divas because Grace reminded her of one, and some early

Rolling Stones because it ought to be familiar to a shy former frigate midshipman.

'How much longer before dinner?' queried Sienna, glancing at the clock. Ten past eight. She glanced at the ceiling.

'About fifteen minutes,' said Rudy dryly, following her gaze. 'Another quandary?'

'Yes.' Lex had said he'd join them when he was done. He hadn't joined them, ergo he wasn't done. But she wanted him to be. 'Think I should go and tell Lex we're almost ready to eat?'

'Yes,' said Rudy.

'He had a lot of work to get through,' she said with a twinge of guilt. 'He said he'd be down when he'd be done.' Lex's foremost stipulation regarding their current living and working situation was that the work had to get done, regardless. He might as well have been talking to the moon for all the attention she'd paid to his request.

'Then we'll send a dinner tray up,' said Rudy.

'You're right,' she said to Rudy. 'I shouldn't disturb him.'

But deep down inside a battle began raging. Because she wanted to disturb him. She wanted to march upstairs and demand he come downstairs and eat with them. Not for his sake, she realised with brutal honesty, but for hers.

She wanted his reassurance that he hadn't forgotten her so quickly. That even when he worked he held the thought of her close. She didn't know where it had come from, this constant need for reassurance as to his affections, this constant need for his attention. She remembered her mother behaving exactly the same way with her father.

The thought terrified her.

'I'll set the table,' she said, dredging a smile up from

somewhere. 'For three,' she said next. 'And I vote we eat in the dining room.'

'You loathe the dining room,' muttered Rudy, shooting her a sharp glance. 'You never set foot in there if you can avoid it.'

'I will confess to being somewhat daunted by its formality,' she replied airily. 'It's not a relaxing room. Tonight, however, you and Grace will be there and I'm feeling relaxed enough and contrary enough to make that rotten room work for me.'

'Candles help,' offered Rudy and reddened when both Sienna and Grace stared at him in astonishment. 'You'll find them in the middle left-hand drawer of the sideboard. If you want them, that is—it makes no difference to me. Cutlery's in the top drawer. Glassware is to the right.'

'The man buys candles,' Sienna murmured, and to Grace, 'Did you know he was a romantic? Because I didn't.'

'I suspected he was,' replied Grace. 'The strong, silent, creative types often are.'

'Maybe you should offer him another beer,' said Sienna. 'Maybe he'll suggest a moonlight sail.'

'I'm all for it,' murmured Grace. 'Maybe I'll offer him *two* beers.'

Rudy sent the pair of them a level, thoughtful stare, and Sienna just knew that retaliation wasn't far away. 'Right, then. I'll be in the dining room making it habitable if you need me. Not that you will.' She had to pass by Rudy on the way out. She couldn't resist stopping and laying a hand on his shoulder, her expression as solemn as she could get it with thoughts of Grace trying to tempt Rudy into even more romantic behaviour running through her mind. 'Good luck, sailor. Make us proud.'

* * *

Grace eyed Sienna's retreating form with a mixture of affection and concern. She didn't know the younger woman particularly well, but she knew enough about womankind to know that something was on Sienna's mind. One didn't need to be a telepath to predict what that something might be.

But first things first.

'At ease, sailor,' she said to Rudy with a disarming smile. Never mind the nit-picking, Rudy had shown a surprising sensitivity to Sienna's increasingly reflective silences. Woeful social skills aside, he'd been surprisingly adept at keeping the mood festive when Sienna's smiles had faltered. Grace liked that about him. She liked a lot of things about this man. 'I may have suggested that second beer, but that doesn't mean you're obliged to drink it. I can recognise a no as well as the next person.'

Rudy looked down at his hands and Grace suppressed a disappointed sigh. For a moment there she thought she'd seen a wanting in his eyes, a heated need that had made her hopeful. Not confident, but hopeful.

And then he looked up and speared her with his bright blue gaze and there was no mistaking the desire in his eyes this time. 'I'll have another stout,' he said gruffly.

Grace's movements weren't always languid and sexy. Grace could move fast when she wanted to. Where the *hell* was the stout?

'Bottom shelf of the drinks fridge, a couple of rows in.' This from Rudy.

'Got it.' Phew! Right. No need to rush. Breathe in, breathe out. Where the hell was her poise? She straightened up, turned around, and tucked a stray strand of auburn hair only marginally streaked with grey back where it belonged. The ground trembled beneath her feet, but she made it to the bench and set the beer directly in front of the only man to ever take her breath away without even trying.

'Thank you,' he said with a slow, sweet smile that promised heaven if she didn't die of asphyxiation first.

'You'll let me know when you want another one?' she croaked.

'Maybe once we're on the boat. We need to have dinner first.'

Dinner. Right. 'Yes.' Grace had temporarily lost track of her surroundings, but recognition was coming back fast. Dinner. Here. With Sienna. The increasingly melancholic Sienna. Grace looked to the ceiling, much as Sienna had done earlier, and narrowed her eyes. 'What about Alex?'

'What about him?' said Rudy.

'The man has to eat some time this evening. He may as well do it with us. Besides, Sienna wants him to come down. How do we go about getting him here? Does coercion work?'

'Not usually,' said Rudy.

'Bribery?'

'With what?'

'What about prompting a spot of self-reflection about what a work-obsessed, neglectful ass he's being?' she suggested.

'That might work,' said a voice from the doorway, and Grace looked up, embarrassment warring with pleasure at the sight of Lex entering the room. He looked freshly showered, shaven of jaw, and altogether as dangerous to womankind as his reputation suggested in his white dinner shirt and formal grey trousers. Sienna had her work cut out for her with this one, no doubt about it. Good thing the girl was up to the task. 'Evening, Alex. How lovely to see you again.'

'Always a pleasure to see you too, Grace,' he said dryly. 'How did the ice cream turn out?'

'It needed champagne.'

Lex looked to Rudy for clarification. Rudy shook his head. 'Your personal assistant turned a perfectly good glass of French champagne into a frothing, bubbling mess.'

'Ah, yes. The Spider. It's one of Sienna's specialities. She usually uses ginger beer.'

'She's a culinary heathen,' said Rudy. 'Next thing you know she'll be eating spaghetti from a tin.'

'Only when sitting in a tent,' said Lex. 'You should see what she does with marshmallows. Where is she, by the way?'

'In the dining room, setting the table,' replied Grace. 'She did wonder about setting a place for you too, but I think she decided against disturbing you.'

'She could have disturbed me.'

'She does disturb him,' murmured Rudy, sotto voce.

'Excellent. I do like a man who isn't all about the work. Tell me, Alex. Do you always dress for dinner or is this a special occasion?'

'I always dress for ice cream,' said Lex, and Grace beamed at him.

'I swear you've all gone ice-cream mad,' muttered Rudy. 'Can someone please tell me what is wrong with chocolate?'

Sienna found the candles and the cutlery in the sideboard and began to collect up the pieces she needed. The table-ware, like everything else in the room, screamed of subtle elegance and no shortage of money. Maybe that was why she never felt comfortable in here, she thought wryly. Maybe the visual confirmation of Lex's wealth rammed home her relative lack of it just that little bit too hard.

Give away most of your money, Lex, so I don't feel inferior.

Drop everything and pay attention to me. Only me. To hell with the work and to hell with anything you might want.

Love me and all my insecurities and maybe one day, some day, I might be brave enough to love you back.

'Aren't you the prize?' she muttered to herself as she lay three sets of cutlery in place and turned to go and get side plates from the kitchen.

She wasn't alone. Lex stood leaning against the door frame, his smile warm but his eyes sharp. 'I wouldn't say prize, exactly. Sometimes I can get downright neglectful of the people who matter to me the most.'

His generosity shamed her. 'I wasn't talking about you. I was talking about me.'

'Ah. Self-reflection,' he murmured as he started towards her looking elegant, confident, and dangerously unpredictable. 'Nasty beast. I had a little moment of it myself not fifteen minutes back, when I looked at the clock, looked at the work, and realised that I'd rather be down here with you. What prompted yours?'

'Silver-plated forks.'

'Kinky. Care to elaborate?'

'No.' Sienna busied herself by looking for matches to light the candles with. She found them in the same drawer she'd found the candles. 'Did you get your work finished?'

'Not all of it.'

Not what Sienna wanted to hear. 'Lex, I'm sorry about

interrupting the work today. I shouldn't have done it. I should have left the personal things—relationship things—for later. I know it wasn't right of me.'

'Did you hear me complaining?'

'Well, not *then*,' she said. 'But what about now? You said there was more to do.'

'I've sent half of it to the London office,' he said. 'It'll be done overnight by someone else and faxed through ready for me tomorrow morning. London works when we sleep. It's one of the benefits of being in different time zones. Relax, Sienna. The work will get done.'

'My mother used to do this,' she said faintly.

'Do what?'

'Ask for too much. Want more of my father's time. Always more.'

'For heaven's sake, Sienna, you are not your mother!' Lex swore fiercely and regarded her bleakly. 'You're *you*, and I've never known a woman to ask for less. So if you want something of me, *ask*. And watch me try and move heaven and earth to see that you get it.'

Not like her father. So not like her father.

'Would you care to join us for dinner?' she asked tentatively, knowing the moment for yet another tiny victory over the past on her part. 'I think it's going to be fun. Lots of fun. It involves—'

'You,' he murmured.

'—a meal,' she countered, 'which Rudy and Grace have generously prepared, followed by an hour or two unwinding in the luxury billiards room to your right and drinking the rotgut of your choice—'

'Cognac,' he whispered with his lips to her ear as his

arms came around her, wrapping her in warmth. 'It's called cognac.'

'It's also likely to involve you sending Rudy and Grace out on a mission to collect some obscure bottle of wine that you don't actually want shortly thereafter. They'll use *Angelina* for transport, possibly *Mercy Jane*, and I really don't think we should wait up.'

'And then what?'

Sienna smiled and surrendered to the moment and to the urge to wrap her arms around his neck. 'Then I guess we go to bed.'

They made it through dinner and billiards and cognac. They saw Rudy and Grace off on the *Mercy Jane*. They made it to Lex's room, with its Italian leather sofas and its big plush bed. They managed to get naked and into the bed and thoroughly entwined in each other's arms. And then they slept.

Sienna woke the following morning to Lex entering the room bearing a tray with two steaming cups of what smelt like coffee on it. He wore a white business shirt and tailored trousers and couldn't have signalled more clearly if he'd shouted that work was on his morning agenda.

'What time is it?' she said sleepily.

'Twenty to six,' he said cheerfully.

'That would be why my eyes don't want to work.' Clearly there were some kinks in this sleeping-in-each-other's-beds business that would have to be ironed out. 'Do you always wake up this early?'

Lex nodded.

'And this cheerful?'

'Usually.'

'Ugh.' Sienna closed her eyes at the injustice of it all. 'You're a morning person.' She, on the other hand, was not.

'You think you've got problems,' he said and she reopened her eyes to find him setting the coffees on the bedside table beside her and then propping the tray against the wall. 'I used to be a lover of some repute. I didn't deliberately cultivate that reputation, mind, but I did grow fond of it. There were certain standards I felt obliged to live up to, and live up to them I did. I never took a woman to bed only to fall asleep. It simply wasn't done.' He sighed heavily and took a seat on the side of the bed. 'And then I took up with you.'

'It might not be me,' she protested, the smell of coffee rousing her to action. She sat up and tucked the sheet firmly around her before propping her pillow against the bed head and leaning back against it. 'You've never actually shared a house with a lover before. Maybe it takes the need for sex on a nightly basis right out of you. Not that I'm complaining, mind. I like to sleep on occasion. You can call me Maverick.'

He handed her the coffee in his hand with unconscious courtesy and reached for the one on the table.

Sienna took a sip and grimaced, not at the flavour, which was perfect, but at the temperature of the brew. 'Hot.'

'I know it's early but I have to go upstairs for a while,' he said. 'I need to resource the capital for this bid and most of it's coming from Wall Street. Two hours on the phone, three at the most, and then I'll be able to hand almost all of the work over to the London office.'

Oh, yeah. The bid. Sienna rubbed her hands over her face and tried to move smoothly from sleepy bed partner to efficient PA. 'You want me to come up now too?'

Lex smiled as he strode towards the door. 'Normal time is fine.'

Which meant nine. 'I'll be there. Ready to work. Possibly clothed. You'll see.'

CHAPTER TEN

'MARRY me,' murmured Lex a week later as they lay sprawled together on the lounge in the drawing room eating home-made French frou-frou food and watching a remake of *Pride and Prejudice* on the television. It was after ten on a Friday evening, maybe after eleven, and Sienna was wearing pyjamas in the form of a grey singlet top and baggy white cotton trousers. Lex's pyjama bottoms were pale blue and white striped and his chest was bare. The day's work had been done, they were well into the play part of the evening. Mr Bingley had just proposed to Jane. Sienna was undeniably happy with her lot.

At least, she had been until Lex had uttered those two little words guaranteed to make her tremble, and not in squirming anticipation. She looked from Lex to the TV screen and back again. No need to panic. Maybe he was just having a little fantasy interlude with one of the Misses Bennetts. Maybe he was playing the film critic and attempting to distil the theme of the story down to two words that started with something other than P.

But then he looked at her, his eyes dark and his expression brooding, and spoke those words again.

'Marry me.'

'What?'

'You heard.'

'Yes, but—' Lex looked away and Sienna felt her heart constrict. 'You're serious.'

'Yes. That's also all you have to say to make this happen, by the way. *Yes.* I particularly liked the way the very sweet Jane Bennett just said, "Yes, yes, a thousand times, yes". Not a *but* in sight. Makes a man feel wanted.'

'Keep watching,' she said. 'You might pick up a thing or two about delivering a successful marriage proposal. There's usually mention of love. Ardent love, tempered by the utmost respect. These words are often delivered with an appealing lack of confidence, possibly even a very sexy stutter. Even if you are as rich as Croesus.'

'You've seen this movie before,' he said.

'Oh, yes.'

'You do realise that both the book and the screenplay were written by women.'

Sienna eyed him narrowly.

'I'm just saying…'

'Your chances of hearing that *yes* are so very low right now,' she told him darkly.

'But there is a chance of it,' he said with no little satisfaction. 'We've established that the offer is sound.'

'Lex, I—' She didn't know what to say that wouldn't hurt him.

'Would it help if I told you how much I love you?' he offered quietly, and when she met his gaze she realised that, although his smile was teasing, his eyes were deadly serious. 'You were right. I may have overlooked that part earlier.'

Sienna ducked her head as tears pricked at her eyes. Served her right for asking for something she didn't know what to do with. 'How can you be sure that this isn't just infatuation?' she said shakily.

'Because I love being with you. Always have, always will. Because I know you. Because there's a place for you inside of me and I want you there.'

Siena closed her eyes.

'Sienna, do you love me?'

It felt like it. If the pain in her heart was anything to go by. Her tears began to fall in earnest.

'Would it be so bad, being married to me?'

'No.' Sienna shook her head and wiped her eyes with her fingers, grateful for the curtain of hair that shielded her face from view. Until gentle fingers tucked her hair behind her ear. She heard Lex curse softly. 'I'm sure you'll make some woman very happy.'

'Why not you, Sienna? Why can't I make you happy?'

'What if it doesn't work?' She knew their time in Australia was coming to a close and that she would lose the closeness to him that she craved once they were back in England, but she wasn't ready for this. Not marriage. Not that. Never that. 'What about your wealth? And my lack of it?' What about her inability to commit for fear of failing him? 'We're just not *equal*, Alex. And I need to be.' Sienna knew exactly what happened when monetary inequality soured a marriage. When *any* type of inequality entered a relationship, for that matter. When one gave more than the other. When one loved more than the other. She knew what came of that.

Hope died first. Then courage died. And then the will to live…died.

'I know you're thinking of your parents, Sienna,' said Lex urgently. 'I know their marriage was a disaster, but it was the exception, not the rule. It doesn't have to be like that. It *wouldn't* be like that. We could be happy together. I know we could. All you have to do is believe in yourself and the things you bring to this relationship.'

But self-belief had never been Sienna's strong suit. 'I don't bring much.' A bundle of insecurities and an old stone house in Cornwall that needed more money spent on it than it was worth. 'You could do so much better.'

'Dammit, Sienna, I don't want better. I want you!' Lex pulled away to stare at the screen. So did Sienna. Mr Darcy currently held court, burning it up with his brooding glances, but he had nothing on Lex. When Lex decided to sizzle and brood he could set the drapery on fire.

'All right,' he said after a fraught twenty seconds of silence. 'Do you concede that, apart from the disparity in our wealth, that we're well matched? That we're quite capable of holding our own with each other intellectually, morally, and—' his eyes took on a decided gleam '—sexually? That to all intents and purposes we are equals in those areas?'

'You're playing with words, Lex.'

'I'm taking that as a yes,' he said. 'For my part, I'm willing to concede that I do have much healthier self-esteem than you, and far fewer abandonment issues. However…I'm willing to wager that, give or take a decade or two, you'll finally figure out your own worth and realise that I'm not going anywhere. Problem solved.'

'In a decade or two?'

'I'm a patient man.'

Bemusement began to spread through her. This conversation had taken a distinct turn for the surreal. 'There's still the small matter of your wealth and my lack of it,' she reminded him. 'How do you plan to even that out? Become the philanthropist and give away all your money?'

'I'd really rather not,' he said dryly. 'Although I do know this woman who needs a few hundred million in order to believe in her own worth enough to take a chance and commit to the man who loves her. I could always give it to her. No?' He'd seen the refusal on her face long before she thought to voice it. 'Hell, Sienna. It was worth a try. All right, so we find another way to improve your finances.'

'We're talking a *lot* of improvement,' she said. 'How do you propose I become a megamillionaire overnight?'

'I didn't say overnight,' he said. 'Realistically speaking, I think you need to look at a somewhat longer time frame than that. I'm thinking that with your rapidly growing business acumen and occasional guidance from a very interested party that you could get there inside a decade.'

'I'm having a thought,' she said.

'Does it involve lottery tickets?'

'No.'

'Games of chance?'

'No.'

'Felonious acts?'

'No,' she said, rolling her eyes. 'Maybe I just need to find those paintings. Maybe if I did that, then everything else would fall into place. Money. Self-confidence. Everything.'

'No.' The teasing light in Lex's eyes had disappeared, replaced by a weariness she didn't often see in him. '*Enough* with the paintings, Sienna. You need to stop pinning your hopes on them, devoting your life to looking for them. You need to find some other way to put your past behind you. That train's not coming.'

She knew it. In her heart she knew it. And still she clung to the thought of them the way a dying man clung to the thought of a miracle cure. 'How do you know?'

'Because my mother's been looking for them for the past twelve years on your behalf,' he said curtly. 'She's had Scotland Yard looking, private galleries, private collectors, private investigators, you name them, she's had them looking for those paintings. Adriana's investigation force spans the globe, but she's never heard a whisper. Not one. They're gone, Sienna. All the way gone.'

'She's been looking for them all this time?' Sienna whispered. 'For me?'

'She knows what they mean to you, Sienna. We all do. I'd love for her to find them for you. I'd love for you to find them so that you could rewrite your past and find some comfort there. But I also need to believe that there's a way for you to move forward without those paintings. With love,' he said quietly. 'With me.'

'I can't,' she said quietly. *Pathetic cowering weakling.* 'I'm so sorry, Lex. You're the finest man I know. Generous, and beautiful, and…beloved. But I just can't.'

Sienna slept badly that night and she slept alone. Surrounded by space, bereft of warmth, she dreamt of loss and of loneliness. Of Lex and a life without him. She lay there in the half light of dawn, her pain a living thing as she remembered the desolation in Lex's eyes when she'd refused his offer of marriage and the hollowness he'd left behind when he'd stood and left the room without another word.

The one person in her life who'd never once let her down and she'd refused everything he had to offer because she would not allow herself to believe that someone like him could want someone like her.

Pathetic cowering weakling. Her father's words haunted her. Cut at her.

Defined her.

At seven-thirty Sienna abandoned all pretence of sleep, pushed back the bedcovers, and headed to the west-wing breakfast room, praying that Rudy had delivered the coffee already and that Lex would be nowhere in sight.

The coffee was in evidence, she could smell it before she'd even entered the room. One down. But Lex was there too, and why wouldn't he be? It was his coffee. His house.

'Morning,' she said, wishing herself far, far away. Wishing that she could somehow turn back time and make everything all right between them. Because it wasn't all right. It was all wrong. And she had no idea how to proceed from here.

He'd showered and shaved this morning, but that was where his concession to orderliness ended. His olive-coloured T-shirt was an old one. His steel-grey workman's trousers had seen better days. The colour matched the colour of his eyes. His eyes made her nervous.

'Morning,' he said smoothly. 'Sleep well?'

She hadn't and he knew it. She figured it for one of those rhetorical questions that didn't need an answer. 'You look dressed for dirt,' she said instead.

'Rudy and I are heading to the boatyard soon. We're building a boat together.' He regarded her with those watchful, measuring eyes. 'You're welcome to come along.'

'No. I—no,' she said awkwardly, heading for the coffee. The sooner she had coffee in hand, the sooner she could leave. 'Thank you. I just—no.' How on earth was she supposed to extricate herself from his life when she was so deeply enmeshed in it?

'You think I'm going to let you go, don't you?' he said mirthlessly. 'Just like that? Just because of one minor setback in our negotiations? I thought you knew me better than that, Sienna. You should have known that come this morning I'd have another offer on the table.'

Sienna fumbled with the coffee pot, cursing as it sloshed over the rim of the cup and onto the floor. Rudy would not be pleased. She set the coffee down and reached for a napkin.

'Leave it,' he said curtly.

She left it. Which left her standing there clutching a napkin in one hand and a coffee in her other. 'What kind of offer?' she said hesitantly. She couldn't deal with another marriage proposal right now. She really couldn't.

'I still want you by my side,' he said. 'That's non-negotiable as far as I'm concerned. Marriage is somewhat more negotiable. We don't necessarily have to marry, although I will reiterate that I would prefer to. It's easier on the children, wouldn't you agree?'

'Children?' she echoed.

'Ours,' he said blithely. 'As for the paintings, I'm prepared to throw considerable time and resources into helping you look for them. Maybe you *will* turn up something that my mother has missed. I figure I can take a month off work, starting from when we leave here, to help you look for them. With all that I am. All that I have. If you really think those paintings will make a difference to your past and to our future, then I'll help you look for them.'

'Lex—'

'Think about it.' He came to stand in front of her and

leaned down to press a light kiss against her unresisting lips. 'That's all I'm asking you to do. Just think about it.' His smile turned rueful. 'Think about it and don't say no.'

Sienna thought about Lex's latest offer all the way back to her room. She should have realised that he would find a way to reopen negotiations. That he would come up with what sounded on the surface like a wholly reasonable compromise—one that nonetheless moved him inexorably closer to getting what he wanted. She'd been watching him in action all week with the takeover bid. At the end of last week she'd have bet money she couldn't afford to lose that the Scorcellinis would decline his offer. But they hadn't. Lex was good at negotiating his way through difficult situations. At turning 'no's into 'maybe's and 'maybe's into 'yes's.

At making people believe.

She *wanted* to find a way to overcome her fears. For Lex. For herself. She badly wanted the scars of her past to stop determining her future. She wanted to understand what had made her mother so fragile that she'd taken her own life. What fundamental flaw pushed a person down that path? What flaw inside her father had made him treat his wife and child so badly? What flaw inside *her* had made them leave her without a second thought? Only someone who'd lived through those years with her parents would know the answers to those questions. Someone who'd lived in the house and witnessed it all. Someone like Elsie.

Elsie had left her too, but Sienna didn't want to dwell on that.

With a little more effort she might be able to find Elsie and talk to her. About the paintings. And about the past.

She needed to see if Maggie Cameron of 42 Aldersley Road, Hornsby, had her phone number listed in the directory.

She did.

Moments later, with Elsie's letter in hand, Sienna had dialled the number and started to pace. The phone rang once. Twice. Five times.

'Hello?' said a woman's voice she didn't recognise. The accent was Australian. The voice sounded elderly. Maggie Cameron, she presumed.

'Hi,' said Sienna hurriedly. 'Ah, hello. I'm not sure if you can help me, and I do apologise for disturbing you if you can't, but I'm trying to find a Mrs Elspeth Blaylock.'

There was a long pause, and then the woman spoke again. 'Who is this?'

'Sienna. Raleigh. Elspeth used to work for my family in Cornwall years ago. I'm in Sydney at the moment and I have your current address written on the back of one of her letters. I got your name from your neighbour, and your number from the book…' Sienna closed her eyes and cursed herself for not being better prepared. 'Her name's Elsie. Elsie Blaylock.'

'Yes, dear. I know. This is Margaret, her sister. But I'm sorry, Sienna. Elsie passed away some twelve years ago. You might remember that she came home to look after me? Turned out that she was the one who was ill.'

'I'm sorry,' Sienna mumbled. 'I'm so sorry. I didn't realise.'

'You're Mary's girl,' said the voice.

'Yes.'

'The one who used to sit in Elsie's kitchen and make pastry snails and butterflies.'

'Yes. That's me.' Sienna fought back unexpected tears. 'I'm so sorry to trouble you. I just thought…well…it would have been nice to see her again, that's all.'

'Elsie would have liked that you called her,' said her sister. 'She used to talk about you all the time. She'd have packed you up and brought you back here with the rest of her belongings if she could have. She never could countenance the way your parents treated each other. Or you, for that matter. "Such a dear little thing," ' she used to call you. "Such a dear and loving little girl." '

Sienna's vision blurred. She could feel herself clutching the letter in her hand; she just couldn't see it any more.

'I swear she used every trick in the book to try and convince her doctor to let her go to Mary's funeral, but she was far too ill to travel by then,' said the voice. 'She had to make do with sending a card. She wrote you a letter too, as I recall. Fretted over it for days, but finally it went in the post.'

'I don't remember receiving it,' Sienna said shakily. 'I don't remember much about those few months at all.'

'Ah, well. You were so young, see? Such terrible things to happen to someone so young. I wouldn't fret one little bit over not remembering that letter. Elsie wouldn't want you to fret,' said the voice. 'She'd have been so pleased that you called. She'd have loved to see you again.'

'I—thank you,' said Sienna. 'I'd have loved to see her again too.'

Sienna ended the call on a wave of emotion. She placed the letter gently on the bed and turned to stare unseeingly out at that million-dollar harbour view, her arms wrapped around her waist, holding her feelings in, keeping others out. She was still standing there when Lex walked in some time later. It could have been one minute later, it could have been ten. She glanced at the clock. Ten past eight. Make that closer to twenty minutes. She gathered herself together with a start. 'I thought you and Rudy were heading out?'

'We are. But Rudy invited Grace to meet us for lunch. She wants to know if you'd like to join us. She thought she could drop by and pick you up on the way.' Lex's sharp gaze went from her to the letter on the bed. 'May I?' he said.

Sienna nodded.

He crossed to the bed and picked it up, scanning it fast. 'You called her?'

'Yes.'

'To ask her if she knew anything about the paintings?'

'More or less.'

'And?'

'She's dead. I spoke to her sister.'

'What did her sister have to say?'

'Nothing much. Nothing about the paintings. She mentioned a letter…a letter Elsie wrote to me after my mother's death. I think I'll try and find it. Not because there'll be anything about the paintings in it because I doubt there will be. But I'd still like to find it.'

'Want some help?' he said quietly. Different offer from his earlier one. Same unwavering support.

'Yes.' It was that or walk away from him and she couldn't do it. She just couldn't do it. 'Will you come to my house in Cornwall with me when we get home? My mother's belongings are there, up in the attic. That's where Elsie's letter will be—if my father didn't throw it out.'

'I'll come,' he said gently.

'For a month?'

'Yes.'

'And help me look for the paintings?'

'If that's what you want.'

Sienna nodded and looked away. She didn't deserve this man. Not his support. Not his love. 'Tell Grace I'll give her a call later,' she said shakily.

'You'll come to lunch?'

'Yes.' He gave so much. She gave so very little back. She could at least join him for lunch. She'd be fine by lunchtime. 'Excuse me. I'd better go and have that shower.'

She left him standing there as she made her way to the bathroom, shed her pyjamas and stepped beneath the spray of a showerhead set to stinging. She felt the tears she'd been holding at bay start to swallow her and she let them come, silent, choking sobs of despair. The water wasn't hot enough; the water didn't burn nearly as much as the pain in her heart. She wanted it steaming, scalding.

The shower door opened abruptly.

Lex.

He saw her face; he saw her tears. 'We'll go to Cornwall,' he said abruptly. 'Paintings or no paintings, you can find your way through this, Sienna. I know you can.' He stepped into the shower beside her, fully clothed, and held her while she wept.

CHAPTER ELEVEN

THE coast of Cornwall in the summertime could be picture perfect, what with its hidden coves and tiny villages nestled atop rugged grey cliffs. Cornwall in February, on the other hand, could be bleak, windswept, miserable and bitterly cold. It was February now, and the attic in Sienna's crumbling manor house didn't afford quite as much protection from the gale that had blown in as she'd have liked. There was a roof. There were damp stone walls all around her and a window that didn't quite fit its rotting wooden frame any more. There were boxes.

A whole row of damp and mouldy boxes that Sienna and Lex had yet to look through.

'I think your roof leaks.' The mildness of Lex's delivery was a masterful example of frustration kept on a very tight leash. He'd said very little about the sorry state of the house. His eyes had said plenty though. He was gearing up for a reckoning, an offer to fix things, probably a health and safety lecture. She didn't want to hear any of it. 'And I think I've found a box of condolence cards,' he added.

Sienna clambered her way over the refuse of her mother's life until she reached Lex's side. She stripped off her gloves and tucked them under her arm, straightened the woollen beanie hat on her head, delved into the box, and opened up one of the cards. Bingo.

'Where do you want them?'

'The kitchen.' It was warmer in the kitchen. Soothing cups of tea could be made in the kitchen. There was gin in the kitchen and a girl never knew when a shot might come in handy.

They'd been home two days, during which time they'd opened up the house, aired the rooms, and shopped for groceries in the village. For all his wealth and the pampering that usually went with it, Lex seemed to be enjoying living life in the rough. He fitted, whether it be up here in the attic with cobwebs in his hair or naked in her bed rousing her with kisses and caresses she was powerless to resist. No Rudy, no pampering, no trappings of wealth. He didn't need them. He fitted *her*.

Two hours later, Sienna sat at the kitchen table with the woodstove throwing welcome heat and the ancient light fittings throwing as much light on the situation as they could, aided in their task by the bronze-based lamp Sienna had brought in from the dining room.

'How old is the wiring in this place?' murmured Lex.

'Older than the ark,' she said dryly. 'And before you nobly refrain to comment any further on the state of the wiring, yes, it needs replacing. It's on the list.'

'That would be the list on the side of the fridge,' he said.

'Yes.'

'That's a long list.'

'I live for challenge.'

Lex's gaze slid to the piles and piles of musty, water-stained condolence cards on the table in front of them and then to the number of cards still in the box. 'This is a good thing.'

'Here's one from your aunt Sophie,' said Sienna. 'With Deepest Sympathy… I think I like the simple cards best. The ones that stay far, far away from promises of heavenly bliss and a better place.' Sienna did better with this task when she concentrated on the myriad ways the greeting card companies portrayed death rather than the names and handwriting of the people who had known and loved her mother.

'I like this one.' Lex held up a card with a picture of an English bulldog in an armchair on the front. 'It's from the secretary of the Cressingdon Rotary Club.'

'It *is* a nice change from lilies,' said Sienna. She glanced down into the box and sighed. 'Anyone for gin?'

'Gin will make you morbid,' he said.

'I'm already there. I'm hoping gin will give me the fortitude to keep going.'

'Have some ice cream instead.'

'I would, but a certain yacht-building, frou-frou cooking *fiend* has spoilt me for all other ice cream but his.' Sienna sighed heavily. So much for Lex doing remarkably well living without the trappings of wealth. Sienna was having withdrawal symptoms. 'I miss Rudy.'

'Half of these haven't even been opened,' muttered Lex. 'This one's a letter. Looks like it's from your father. It's addressed to your mother.' His gaze met hers, wary and concerned. 'Want me to read it?'

'No, I'll do it.'

Lex handed it over reluctantly, as if he could sense her sudden dread. 'Sienna, you don't have to do this.'

But that was where he was wrong. 'Yes,' she said

quietly. 'I do.' More than ever she wanted to understand her parents' love-hate relationship. Dissect it, understand it, be free of it.

'I'll put the kettle on,' said Lex.

'Thanks.'

The kettle had boiled and Lex had made instant coffee for them both by the time Sienna had worked her way through both pages of closely written prose. 'Anything interesting?' he asked as she set the letter aside and he set the coffee in front of her.

'No. Nothing to do with the paintings, at any rate. My father was explaining why he'd been bedding one of my mother's acquaintances. Apparently my mother drove him to it. She wasn't earthy enough. Passionate enough. He called her a porcelain doll and just as cold. It was a hurtful letter. He'd written it that way deliberately. I'm glad she never read it.' She picked up her coffee and sipped, grateful for the bracing hit of caffeine on a body that was running low.

'That's not how I remember Mary,' said Lex. 'Beautiful, yes. With porcelain skin. Gracious and graceful and sometimes a little reserved around people she didn't know. Sometimes there was a sadness about her, but she wasn't cold.'

'No.' Sienna slid him a grateful glance and a watery smile. 'She wasn't cold at all. He didn't love her, not properly. Not the way she should have been loved.' She tossed the letter aside and reached for the next envelope. 'He didn't love anyone.'

'Do you know much about your father's background, Sienna?' said Lex gently.

'You mean the starving artist living in his garret and

the beautiful heiress who discovered him and then proceeded to fall in love with him?' Another condolence card not from Elsie. 'I know enough.'

'Adriana once told me that your father's mother had died giving birth to him. And that he'd been raised by a father who'd found solace in a bottle and given little thought to feeding or clothing the boy who'd killed his wife. Your father grew up hard, Sienna. He grew up without love. Hate and envy had a very strong hold on him. One he couldn't shake.'

'Is that supposed to make me understand why he did the things he did?'

Lex shrugged and sent her a rueful smile. 'Does it?'

'No,' she muttered and reached for another card. 'He was so…destructive. The more she gave, the more he hated her. If he didn't love her, why couldn't he have just let her be? He never let her *be*. He broke her. And then he killed himself because he couldn't live with what he'd done. I don't *understand*.'

'Maybe you don't *need* to understand,' countered Lex gently. 'Maybe knowing that you're not like him is enough. Because you're not like him, Sienna. Or your mother, for that matter. You're stronger than they were. You're the strongest person I know. You kept going, never mind the wounds they inflicted on you with their neglect. Your resilience amazes me, your willingness to believe the best of people humbles me. After all you've been through you still look for sunshine, even after the bleakest of moments. Why do you think I fell in love with you?'

Sienna felt her insides melt at his words. She'd spent most of her life feeling abandoned and confused. Scared of intimacy. Scared of turning out like her parents: over-dependent or abusive, suicidal, take your pick. But Lex didn't think she was any of those things. He thought her strong.

The notion staggered her. Her, strong.

They found Elsie's letter towards the bottom of the box. In it Elsie poured out her love, concern and regret that she wasn't able to attend the funeral. She offered advice on whom of Mary's friends and family young Sienna could trust and turn to for advice. Adriana Wentworth's name was at the top of her list. She spoke of Margaret, her own sister, and said that if ever Sienna phoned or came to visit and Elsie wasn't there, then Margaret would take care of her. She told Sienna never to forget that there were people who loved her and that all Sienna had to do was reach out to them and they would be there. She wrote not a single word about Sienna's father even though he'd still been alive at the time. Elsie had been with Mary for twenty years. She'd known that young Sienna would find no comfort there.

There was no mention whatsoever of Elsie's own illness.

The letter made Sienna's eyes water and her heart fill with gratitude towards an old woman who'd tried to steer a young girl through the aftermath of her mother's death from half a world away. Sienna looked up to find Lex staring at her, his jaw clenched and his eyes shadowed. 'There's nothing here about the paintings,' Sienna told him with a weary smile that she couldn't make stick. 'It's just advice to a young girl who's just lost her mother. Good advice,' she added faintly as her eyes filled again.

'Sienna, you don't have to do this,' said Lex gruffly. 'I don't give a damn whether we find these paintings or not. It's you I care about. And I hate what this is doing to you.'

'Hey, people pay good money for therapy like this.'

Sienna tried for lightness and almost succeeded. 'I'm saving a fortune here.'

'You're hurting,' he said. 'And watching you hurt and not being able to do anything about it is killing me.' He stood up, paced the room, back and forth, back and forth. 'Let's get some air. Take a wander around the grounds or a walk along the cliffs.'

'In this weather?' She'd been watching the wind pick up and the rain come down all afternoon, wondering if today would be the day that the roof on this place finally gave up the good fight. Judging by the rattling of the windows and the whistling of the wind there was a very good chance it might be. 'It's a nice idea, don't get me wrong. It's lovely along the cliffs, but right now it's raining *pellets* out there and they're coming down sideways.'

'Exploration is not weather-dependent,' he said, striding to the kitchen door and opening it, only to be driven back a step by an icy north easterly that set china rattling and envelopes flying. 'I see your point,' he said, leaning his shoulder into the door in order to push it closed again. 'You can show me round the inside of the house instead, point out all the things that need fixing or replacing.'

'Are you going to offer to have them all fixed or replaced?' she said, eyeing him as sternly as she could, given that this was the man who loved her and thought her strong.

'I was thinking more along the lines of bypassing the offer altogether and moving straight onto the fixit side of things.'

'You donning a carpenter's belt is an appealing picture,' she said. Very, very appealing. There was something about a handyman multimillionaire who loved her and thought her strong that pushed every one of her buttons and then some. 'But I think I'd rather you gave me your thoughts as we went around as to whether this place was worth fixing up at all. A very clever man once told me to sell the place and cut my losses if I couldn't maintain its upkeep. Maybe it's time I took his advice.'

He looked at her, his expression wry. 'Sienna, no. Some things you have to let go of. The sins of your parents is one of them. They're not your sins. The need for a bunch of paintings to make you rich enough that you can marry me is another. But if you love this house, keep it. There's a solidness here that's worth building on.' He looked around the long-neglected room. 'Maybe you need to investigate the possibilities of taking on a business partner who can provide you with the capital you need to restore this place properly. You could look to opening up the place to paying guests at a later date, if you wanted to. A sympathetic business partner would be amenable to any number of plans for this place, including retaining it as a summer house for the occasional benefit of himself, his life partner, and their offspring.'

Sienna left her seat for the sole purpose of finding a better one on Lex's lap. She put one hand to his heart and her other to his cheek and dropped a gentle kiss on his lips, a kiss that inevitably turned hungry. 'Where exactly might I start looking for this wondrous-sounding business partner, do you think?'

'Oh, you wouldn't have to look far.'

'You're a good man, Alexander Wentworth the Third,' she whispered, twining her arms around his neck and positioning her body for maximum points of contact, never mind their bulky clothing. 'Why don't I start by showing my potential new business partner the master bedroom?' It was warm up in her bedroom, she'd had a fire going in the hearth all afternoon to ward off the chill. 'We can tour the rest of the house later.'

Lex's touch had always brought pleasure and need to Sienna, but this time it brought with it so much more. His touch infinitely gentle as he peeled away her layers of clothing until she was as vulnerable and as naked as the day she was born. His movements hurried as he shed his own clothes thereafter. As if he thought she might change her mind and turn him away, but there was no turning away from this. She couldn't bear to turn away.

She could see their reflections in the gilt-edged mirror over the mantelpiece, Lex so dark and beautiful, every leanly muscled line of his body drenched in perfection, and herself so pale and slender in comparison. She'd inherited her mother's porcelain skin. She had her father's eyes. Her father's words came back to haunt her only this time she tried pushing them away. I'm not pathetic, cowering, and weak. I'm not!

'Tell me what you see,' he murmured, and she shook her head.

'No.'

His smile grew rueful as his gaze met hers in the mirror. 'Want to know what I see?' He didn't wait for an answer. 'I see a six-year-old girl in a pretty pink dress, with a ribbon in her hair halfway up a tree staring down at me and asking me if I'd ever been to the top. I see a twelve-year-old girl so pale and withdrawn she almost broke my heart, and then she saw me heading her way and smiled and broke my heart all over again. I see an eighteen-year-old woman-child in a pale blue dress who trembled in my arms and made me feel like a king. I see the generous and loving woman who holds my heart, and I see our future and it's bright with love and riches that have nothing to do with money. Tell me you see it too.'

I'm not pathetic cowering and weak. I'm not! She repeated the litany over and over in her mind but she wasn't there yet. She still couldn't bring herself to take that last step. Sienna turned her back on the mirror and the picture they made and drew his head down towards hers, praying that it would be enough, that he would not turn away from her. 'I see only you.'

The eye of the storm hit at around midnight, rattling the windows and the roof and funnelling icy gusts of air down the chimney, sending the cinders flying. Lex got up to check the fire, Sienna got up to go upstairs to the attic and check on the roof.

'No,' said Lex when she declared her intentions. 'It's not safe up there right now. It'll have to wait until the storm passes. Check it tomorrow. Get some local roofers in to look at it tomorrow. They can put together a quote on the replacement cost while they're there.' Not a man to cool his heels once a concession had been made, Lex. Not a man to take no for an answer and leave it at that. She loved that about him. She needed that from him. 'Come back to bed,' he murmured, his eyes darkening. 'I guarantee I'll make it worth your while.'

'I have a better idea,' she said, with every intention of taking control of this lovemaking session right from the start, and, what was more, *keeping* it. 'Why don't you let me make it worth yours?'

* * *

The view from her bedroom windows the following morning wasn't a pretty one. Long-neglected trees had lost branches, the dovecote lay in pieces on the ground, and the stable roof had fallen in and taken part of the stable wall with it.

'It could have been worse,' she murmured as Lex came to stand beside her. 'I could have had a horse.'

'True,' he said. 'There's something sticking out of the wall.'

There *was* something sticking out of the wall. Some sort of thin wooden-pallet-sized container. Probably just insulation. One tiny little patch of insulation. In a stable wall. Sienna looked harder. Then she looked at Lex to see if he was thinking what she was thinking. His eyes were narrowed, his brow furrowed. 'Want to go down for a closer look?' he said finally.

'I think so,' she said, trying hard to emulate Lex's calm. Paintings came in pallet-sized thin wooden containers these days. Rembrandts didn't, to be sure. But some did.

'Now?' he said.

'I think so.'

'Yes,' he said next. 'I think so too.' And matched her, speed for speed, in his rush to get dressed.

'There's a Monet in my stable wall,' said Sienna some ten minutes later as they stood amidst the rubble and stared at the thin wooden box sitting snugly between the outer stonework wall and inner stable-box lining.

'No, there *might* be a Monet in your stable wall,' countered Lex calmly, though if ever a box looked as if it contained a couple of paintings, this was it. As a child he'd adored the excitement and anticipation of a treasure hunt.

As a man he still enjoyed the hunt, but the stakes here were too high and he wasn't talking about a bunch of priceless paintings.

He thought he'd been so clever, agreeing to help her look for the missing paintings. It had bought him time to show her what a life with him would be like, given her more time to get used to the idea of marrying him. It had kept her by his side. Somewhere along the way Sienna was supposed to have come to the conclusion that she loved him enough to marry him anyway, and to hell with the paintings.

But she hadn't.

He'd never really expected to *find* the paintings.

He didn't know whether he wanted to find the paintings now. They would make her wealthy in her own right, true enough. They might help her reconcile her past—he didn't really know how that was supposed to work, other than Sienna thought it would help. If finding the paintings gave her the confidence to marry him, good.

If a small part of his brain protested that if Sienna really loved him she wouldn't let herself *be* deterred by financial inequality or a traumatic past, well, he tried to ignore that particular philosophy in favour of working with the one on the table.

'Let's pull it out,' she said, suiting actions to words, but the box didn't move. 'Lex, help me pull it out.'

Her excitement was infectious. Her suppressed impatience conjured up his own. The sooner they knew what was in that damned box, the sooner he could deal with it. He added his strength to hers, but the box was wedged in tight. 'Got a crowbar?' he said. 'And a hammer?'

'All that sort of stuff used to live in the tack room,' she said with an air of dismay as she turned to survey the rear of the stables. 'The good news is that the tack room is still intact. The bad news is that the entrance door is blocked by wreckage from the roof. It's that door on the far left. But there's a window.'

The window proved the way in and shortly thereafter Sienna armed with the hammer, and Lex with the crowbar, headed back towards the box.

Halfway there, Sienna began to grin. Then she began to laugh. 'Does this feel somewhat surreal to you? I feel like Nancy Drew.'

Lex did not feel like Nancy Drew. Lex felt a lot like a tack-room door, one whose world was about to come crashing down around him. But he anteed up and set the crowbar to shifting stones with as much goodwill as he could muster. Minutes later the thin wooden box was free and Sienna lowered it gently to its side on the ground.

'How do you want to do this?' he said.

'Carefully. Maybe there's a latch or a lock. Maybe it'll just swing open.'

But there wasn't and it didn't. The box, if it was a box, had been nailed shut tight. 'I vote we loosen one of the sides with the hammer and then pry it off with the crowbar,' he said. 'Carefully.'

Sienna nodded and he set to work. The join came loose reluctantly but finally Lex had made enough of a crack to lever the claw of the hammer into it and loosen one side of the box. He wedged the crowbar deep into the centre of the crack so that one solid push would pop the side entirely and knelt there, looking to Sienna kneeling in the dirt on the other side of the crate, her clothes dusty and her eyes shining with hope.

'Hey, Nancy,' he said softly, holding out the crowbar towards her. 'Your turn.'

Sienna leaned across and closed her hand over his. Her hand trembled. 'Together,' she said.

'All right.'

Together they pushed on the crowbar and watched the side of the box pop free. Lex looked at Sienna and she at him. 'I can't look,' she said in a shaking voice.

Lex didn't want to. The contents of that box held the key to his future, his and Sienna's, and he hated being at its mercy. 'Together,' he said gruffly.

'All right,' she whispered.

And together they leaned down and peered into their future.

Lex sat back up first. Sienna stayed looking, looking for what he didn't know because there was nothing to see.

'It's empty,' Sienna said in a small voice, and the stricken look in her eyes made his heart bleed and his stomach clench.

'Yes.'

'They're not here.'

'No.'

'There's nothing here.'

'I don't care,' he said fiercely, and at her continued dismay, 'I don't care. The only reason I gave a damn whether those paintings were here or not was because you gave a damn, and because you have it fixed in your head that a marriage between us would fail without them. Well, it *wouldn't* fail, Sienna. The difference in our financial status carries as much weight as we decide to give it, and I give it none. *None!*' Her eyes were huge and she made as if to speak, but he wasn't done yet. 'And if you would just stop *thinking* about our circumstances for a moment and start *feeling* your way through all this, you might just decide that you don't give a damn about the money side of things either.' He looked down at the empty crate and something settled inside him, something bleak and bitter to fill the growing hollowness. 'I can't do this.'

She scrambled to her feet, her hand outstretched towards him, but he couldn't have her near him, didn't want her near him, not now. His need was too strong and so was his despair. 'Alex—

'No!' He backed away fast. 'No, Sienna. I'm sick of watching you dodge commitment to me in favour of wallowing in your past and pinning your hopes on a bunch of paintings we may never find.' He made it to the door without stumbling. He almost kept walking, he needed to keep walking, but there was one last point he needed to make. 'Why can't you pin your hopes on me?'

Sienna watched helplessly as Lex strode away from her, dashed hopes mixing with despair and self-disgust to form a cocktail of rioting emotions. The one that surfaced first was anger. Not at Lex, no, not at Lex. This anger was directed squarely at herself. At her past and her stupid, senseless inability to let go of it. She stared down at the pallet on the ground and the hammer and crowbar lying next to it. The hammer wasn't big enough, she decided, and the crowbar wasn't quite right either. There was an axe in the tack room, maybe that would do the job. She found it a couple of minutes later, and with carnage in mind headed back to the pallet, her anger building with every step she took towards it. She kicked the box for good measure, stamped on it, and finally she raised the axe over her head.

'Hi, Daddy,' she said. 'I hear you in my dreams, in my head, and I'm sick of you. You hear me? I'm sick of listening to you. This is for being a husband no woman deserved.' Down went the axe and bit deep into the box. Wood splintered, but not enough. 'And this is for being a father no child deserved.' Thud went the axe. Crack went the pallet.

One down. But there was still her conflicting feelings for her mother to deal with.

'I'm sorry that you never knew love the way I know it. I'm sorry that you chose the wrong man to give your heart to, but you didn't have to let him break you,' she said, and let the years of anger and grief at her mother's final betrayal begin to build inside her. She started in on the sides of the box this time, swinging the axe in a wide sideways arc, sending the pallet skidding across the dirt. 'I don't care if I never find those bloody paintings, you hear me? I don't want them any more. I don't need them any more. I don't need you.' She set the axe aside and dragged the half-ruined pallet upright to rest against what was left of the wall. She picked up the axe again, hefted it, found a solid two-handed grip. 'I'm very, very angry with you. This…' She raised the axe high. 'This is for leaving me.' And with a frenzy of blows she smashed that box to hell and back.

When she was done…when her breath came in great gasping heaves and sweat stung the corners of her eyes…she dropped the axe to the ground and wiped her face with the sleeve of her shirt, well satisfied with the destruction she had wrought.

'I'm through with you,' she muttered, kicking at a corner chunk of box for good measure. 'Both of you. I won't let you destroy the love I've found.'

And turning her back on the wreckage of her past, she went in search of a future bright with love and filled with riches that had nothing to do with money and everything to do with belief.

She found him on the cliffs, looking every inch the brooding, scowling thief of hearts that he was. He watched her approach but he gave her nothing. Why would he, thought Sienna with a growing sense of panic, when all she'd done lately was reject everything he offered? Too scared to accept his love. Too wrapped up in her past to see the pain she'd been causing him.

But she saw it now. And she wanted it gone.

'I wondered if I'd find you here,' she said as she came up beside him.

He looked at her in silence and the hopelessness and despair in his eyes tore at her soul. The Lex of her childhood had never lost hope. There'd been nothing he couldn't do. *She* had been the child of despair and lost dreams, but she wasn't a child any more. She was a woman. A loving, caring woman, and if the man she loved beyond measure had lost hope, then he would just have to accept some of hers. 'We didn't eat breakfast. I thought you might want a cup of tea, or coffee. Or something.'

'No.'

'Or we could go into the village and have breakfast at the bakery. I hear the pies are very good.'

'No.'

'I'll find something in the cupboard,' she offered next. 'Tinned baked beans on toast. Don't tell Rudy.'

A twisted smile. Not much, but it was something.

'Alex, I have an apology to make. I was hoping to make it over breakfast or at the very least over a cup of coffee in the kitchen, but I'll make it here if I have to. I'll make it anywhere, and I'll make it short. I'm sorry I hurt you with my refusal to believe in your love for me, or in mine for you. I'm sorry it took me so long to realise that all the love I've ever dreamed of was right there in front of me and that it was mine for the taking if only I dared to believe. I didn't mean to hurt you. I never want to hurt you. I'd rather cut out my own heart than trample yours.' Sienna took a ragged breath and straightened her shoulders. 'I know it's a lot to ask, but if you haven't given up on me…if you still want me for your wife…I'd like you to ask me to marry you one last time.' She was trembling by the time she reached the last word. 'If that's what you want.'

'I have no ring,' he said roughly.

'I don't need a ring.'

'I don't have pretty words.'

'You do have pretty words. You can string together the prettiest, most persuasive words I've ever heard. But the ones in your heart are the only ones I want to hear. They're the most beautiful words of all.'

A smile began to bloom in Lex's eyes, a teasing light that chased away the darkness and always had. 'About that bended-knee thing…'

'Alex,' she said warningly. 'We can talk about control issues later. Preferably when we're naked. I love it when we do that. But right now would you mind a great deal if you just got on with your proposal?'

'I can do that,' he said, and his eyes grew vividly intent as he took her hand in his and lifted it to his lips. 'Ready?'

'Ready.' Finally ready. Love had graced her life and she didn't ever intend to let it go.

'Marry me, Sienna,' he said quietly. 'Marry me and fill my heart.'

'Yes,' she whispered joyously. 'A thousand times, yes.'

EPILOGUE

Sydney, Australia—a good day for a christening

'LOOK at her,' cooed Grace, a vision of nautical elegance and sophistication in navy blue trousers, a lightweight cream-coloured tunic, and a red and gold silk scarf tied around her neck just so. A pair of practical navy-blue deck shoes completed the outfit and gave notice to all who sailed these waters that the lady had plans to come aboard. 'Isn't she just the most gorgeous thing you've ever seen?'

'She certainly is,' said Sienna admiringly. She'd opted for white shorts and a deep red T-shirt made from the softest jersey, and she too had traded heels for something with a little more grip. Practical white tennis shoes graced her feet, and her fingers were bare of everything but a dazzling white diamond on her left-hand ring finger, which Rudy could remove over her cold dead body. No scarf for Sienna, just a floppy-brimmed hat and sunglasses. Newly purchased sunglasses, sourced by Georgie and dark enough so that a woman could look where she would and no one would know. No one but Lex, that was. Lex always seemed to know when she was admiring him.

Sienna smiled and raised her hand in greeting as the

sleek and graceful eight-point-two-million-dollar baby, currently manned by a skeleton crew of two—one of whom she'd just been admiring—came slowly in to dock at the Watson's Bay private jetty where she and Grace waited. Engine-powered for the moment, the yacht would unfurl its sails for the first time ever once the current skipper had picked up the rest of his crew and made for open water. Sienna could hardly wait to get on deck and feel her go.

'What did they call her?' she asked Grace. She'd been remiss. She'd been too busy admiring other things on board that there boat to notice her name and now it was half hidden by the jetty.

'Rudy named her.' Was Grace *blushing*? 'Ask him.'

'I will,' murmured Sienna, enjoying the moment even more once she'd made out the words written in slashing black scrawl on the side of the bow. 'Oh, I will.'

The engine purred as the craft slid ever closer towards them. Lex was there, leaning port side, hand outstretched to help them board. First Grace's beach bag and an over-stuffed picnic hamper, then Grace herself, followed by Sienna. Lex grinned, the black bandana keeping his hair in check reminiscent of a somewhat more piratical age. Pirate looked good on him. Always had. Love looked good on him too.

'Grace,' he said, 'gorgeous as always,' and brushed Grace's cheek with his lips.

Sienna's welcome was somewhat more lingering. Clearly his pirate attire had gone to his head.

'Later for you,' she murmured as her body tightened in response to Lex's caress. 'I have to go and pay my respects to the skipper.' She waited until Rudy had cleared the jetty and turned the yacht around and pointed her towards the Pacific, but that was all the reprieve the big man was going to get from her today.

The bridge area gleamed white in the sunlight; the boat wheel a matt-finished masterpiece of low-gleam stainless steel. Below, she would doubtless find an engine room fitted with all the latest in radar, sonar, and communications equipment needed by the intrepid ocean-going sailor as well as a luxury galley, entertaining area, and bedrooms.

'Grace tells me you were the one who named her,' she said airily by way of greeting. 'Dangerous move, what with you being such a romantic and all.' Rudy scowled. Sienna's smile widened, she couldn't help it. She'd missed the big man, missed his gruffness and his cooking. Definitely his cooking. 'Unfortunately, in all the excitement of watching the yacht slide up to collect us, Grace clean forgot to tell me what it was. I'm afraid I was too busy admiring her beauty to notice her name. I do hope I'm not turning into, you know, a male.' Sienna beamed at him for good measure. So far Rudy had been running true to form and hadn't said a word. 'So about that name…Is it romantic? Does it involve chocolate?' Sienna looked up at the shiny new rig; this really was the most beautiful craft she'd ever crewed on. Not that she'd actually *done* any crewing on her yet. 'You didn't call her *Truffle*, did you?'

'She's called the *Gracie Mae*,' muttered Rudy gruffly, ears reddening as he stared straight ahead.

Yes, she was. Sienna smiled at the sky. There wasn't a cloud in it. 'Because she's fast?'

'Because she's all I've ever wanted,' the big man said

simply, and she closed her eyes and breathed in deep and thought Grace a lucky woman. Almost as lucky as Sienna.

'That's so sweet.'

'I hear your nuptials are to be here in Australia,' he said next.

'Yes.' Sienna opened her eyes and turned to smile at Rudy, who was eyeing the high set solitaire diamond on her ring finger with wry resignation. 'No,' she said, pre-empting his request for her to take it off.

'Figured as much,' he said, with the hint of a smile. 'Grace is beside herself at being asked to be your matron of honour.' He cleared his throat. 'I found a giant Bombe Alaska recipe the other day. It needs tweaking, but I figure I can have it sorted by your wedding day. If that's what you wanted for a cake.'

'Rudy, that sounds brilliant.'

Rudy nodded, once, and that was that. Wedding cake sorted. 'Mr Wentworth,' he said in a louder voice. 'Ready on the mainsail. The spinnaker's yours,' he said to Sienna. 'Let's get moving.

'C'mon, my beauty,' Sienna heard him whisper coaxingly as she headed for the foredeck. 'Don't be shy. You've shown them your quality. Now let's show them what you can do.'

Gracie Mae's crew played until well after noon, but finally they slowed and dropped sail and settled down to the business of refuelling their bodies. Grace's picnic basket was a treasure trove of goodies and the galley fridge had been fully stocked. There was home-made triple-cream vanilla ice cream in the freezer section of that fridge. With chocolate chips. Sienna didn't eat it first. She had to make her way past the sandwich platter first. The salmon, rocket and cream cheese with dill on sourdough. The king prawn and Thai salad wraps. And the strawberry, watermelon, rockmelon and lemon mint kebab chasers.

Only after she'd done full justice to the *Gracie Mae*'s maiden feast did she turn her attention to ice cream.

'Rudy, you've outdone yourself,' she murmured after savouring her first taste. 'This is fabulous. I especially like the chocolate chips.'

'They're not chips,' said Rudy. 'They're shavings.'

'Oh. Shavings.' She caught Lex's smirk and hid her own smile. 'Well, they're very good. Mind you, it could do with a little something…more,' she said, eyeing the magnum of champagne Rudy had seemingly conjured out of nowhere.

'Eyes off,' he said. 'This is for *Gracie Mae*.'

'Really?' Sienna winked at Grace. 'Hog.'

'The *boat*,' said Rudy.

'I knew that.'

'There's one in every family.' Rudy's voice was long suffering, but the corners of his eyes had crinkled.

'It seems to me,' said Sienna artlessly, 'that this "smashing of magnums over the bow of the boat" business could well scratch the finish. And that would be a shame. It seems to me, that a lady such as this one would prefer us to pour some bubbles into a fine crystal flute and tip it gently over her bow as everyone aboard her raises their fine crystal flutes full of champagne and whatever other additives seem to be on hand and drinks to her as well. But don't mind me. Just a suggestion.'

'You didn't seriously think that would work, did you?' murmured Lex from behind her, holding two champagne flutes towards her as Rudy headed above deck with his magnum in tow. Lex carried two more champagne glasses in his other hand. 'There's more champagne in the fridge.'

'Watch and learn,' she said with a slow smile guaranteed to drop a man at fifty paces. 'When are you going to make an honest woman of me?'

'Whenever you set the date,' he murmured. 'How long did you say that dress was going to take, again?'

'Six weeks. The dress will be ready in two. We're waiting on the shoes.'

'Couldn't you just choose a different pair of shoes?'

'Not according to Georgie.'

'You mean Georgie of business-suit fame?'

'That's the one.'

'I stand corrected,' he said fervently. 'By all means, wait for the shoes. Feel free to get her to design your entire trousseau.'

'She does have a holistic approach to these things,' said Grace, coming up and deftly commandeering two champagne glasses from Lex. She plucked another from the galley cupboard. 'Wedding plans aside, we seem to have a slight problem with the christening arrangements. Rudy can't quite bring himself to risk the finish.'

'Well, who would?' Sienna smiled innocently.

'He wants us all up on the foredeck,' said Grace as she headed for the hatch.

'Be right there,' said Sienna.

'What? No ice cream?' said Lex as she swiftly set the lid back on the container and set it back in the freezer.

'Not this time. This is Rudy's big moment and I want to do right by him. No ice cream.'

* * *

They stood on the foredeck with blue sky above them and ocean below, and nothing on the horizon but more sea and more sky, and filled five glasses to the brim. Lex began the toasts.

'To the best-laid plans,' he said.

'To dreaming the dream,' said Rudy.

'And following your heart,' said Grace.

And then it was Sienna's turn. She looked to Rudy and to Grace and saw love at play, vivid and strong, never mind that it had found them so late. She looked to Lex, her patient Lex, with his quicksilver eyes and his marauder's soul that had so completely captured hers. He'd showered her torn and tender heart with the sweetest kind of love and she savoured every moment and knew it for a gift, such a priceless, treasured gift, and she gave it back in turn. From her heart back to his, and round and round again. She lifted her glass high and touched it to the others.

'To those who dare to believe.'

* * * * *

SIENNA'S SPIDERS

ADD one scoop of vanilla ice cream
to any tall glass of carbonated beverage:
be it lemonade, cola, creaming soda,
ginger beer, apple cider, or indeed
champagne.

On sale 2nd January 2009

(2-IN-1 ANTHOLOGY)

HER HIGH-STAKES PLAYBOY & SEALED WITH A KISS

by Kristin Hardy

Her High-Stakes Playboy

To retrieve her grandfather's stolen stamps Gwen needs sexy poker player Del's help. But with this rugged risk-taker she could get far more than she gambled on…

Sealed with a Kiss

Gwen's sister Joss will stop at nothing to get the stamps back…especially if it means seducing tall, dark private eye John "Bax" Baxter into helping her !

SHARE THE DARKNESS

by Jill Monroe

FBI Agent Ward Cassidy thinks Hannah is a criminal. And Hannah suspects Ward is working for her murderous ex-fiancé. But when they get trapped in a hot, dark lift for hours, the sensual pull of their bodies tells them all they *really* need to know.

HIDE AND SEEK

by Samantha Hunter

Tired of hiding in the witness protection programme Jennie Snow is ready for a loving – *not to mention sizzling hot* – relationship with co-worker Nathan Reilly. Yet it's soon clear he's got a few steamy secrets of his own…

Available at WHSmith, Tesco, ASDA, and all good bookshops

www.millsandboon.co.uk